THE VAMPIRE WANTS A WIFE

ANDIE M. LONG

This book is a work of fiction. Names, characters, places and incidents are either the product of the author's imagination or are used fictitiously, and any resemblance to actual persons, living or dead, events or locales is entirely coincidental.

No part of this book may be reproduced or transmitted in any form or by any means, electronic or mechanical, including photocopying, recording or by any information storage and retrieval system without the written permission of the author, except for the use of brief quotations in a book review.

Copyright (c) 2017 by Andrea Long

All rights reserved.

Cover by J.C. Clarke. Photo from Adobe Stock.

*This book is dedicated to my past loves:
Buffy the Vampire Slayer, Angel, The Lost Boys,
Charmed, and so many, many more.*

CONTENTS

Chapter 1	1
Chapter 2	11
Chapter 3	25
Chapter 4	37
Chapter 5	53
Chapter 6	61
Chapter 7	69
Chapter 8	79
Chapter 9	89
Chapter 10	95
Chapter 11	109
Chapter 12	121
Chapter 13	125
Chapter 14	141
Chapter 15	155
Chapter 16	167
Chapter 17	175
Chapter 18	183
A DEVIL OF A DATE	191
About the Author	193
Also by Andie M. Long	195

CHAPTER One

Shelley

*A*nother freaking lunatic.

After a year in business running a dating agency, I still got frustrated by pranksters or insane people who wrote out ridiculous application forms. This loser obviously had nothing better to do as he had filled out the entire questionnaire extensively. Most morons put a stupid name like Superman and then followed it up with swear words as the answer to every question. Seeing as this one had made an effort, and it was Monday morning and my coffee hadn't sunk in yet, I decided to sit back and read it. Perhaps I'd print it off for when I wrote my book at the end of my dating agency career, *Confessions of a Matchmaker*.

Name: Theodore Robert Landry
Date of birth: 1 January 1891
Age: 126

Hair: Black
Skin colour: Alabaster
Height: Six feet two inches.
Weight: Perfect.

Any distinguishing features?
I'm a vampyre, so fangs?

Place of Birth:
Goodacres Farm, Withernsea, East Yorkshire

Current address:
The Basement, 27 Sea View Road, Withernsea. (I was thrown out of my place of birth on becoming a vampire. I'm on a quest to win my home back, but currently my duel has not been accepted. They keep sending a policeman around asking me to desist).

Any family history of note:
All deceased, I was the only family member to survive. The rest of my family were drained of their blood. It was difficult at first but it's true time is a healer. I think fondly of them now. It's quite usual for a newly turned vampire to kill their family members by accident.

Favourite food:
A classic O-neg, preferably drunk straight from the source. I note you don't ask blood type on your appli-

cation. That may be something for you to consider for future.

Ideal dating venue:
Can only be after 8pm up until 4am to be on the safe side. A nice, dark environment such as a park, graveyard, nightclub, restaurant (I can eat human food, but it has no calorific value for me) would be ideal.

Reason for Application
I have been trying to find a wife now for several years. I am extremely good looking and have a vast intellect due to my many years on this earth. Unfortunately, when I discuss the fact my girlfriend would have to be turned into a vampire and be my wife long into the eternal light, they leave. Usually rather rapidly. I am therefore reaching out in these modern times to your dating agency. Your tagline promises to find 'your ideal partner'. My ideal partner preferably would be a vampire like myself, complete with no heartbeat, but should you not have such members on your books, a beautiful human lady who is willing to be turned would suffice.

Jesus! I clicked on the attached photograph, fully expecting to see a dick pic but instead there was a picture of a pale-faced God-like creature. He couldn't be real because he was far too fucking hot. It would be a model shot. I quickly did a Google image search of the photo, but nothing came back. Hmm, interesting.

At that point the door burst open, making me upend my still hot coffee down my front. I jumped up and down doing the dance of the scalded, wafting my top and holding it away from my skin. "Oh, God. Oh fucking God. That's hot. That is fucking hot."

"Oh my, he is fucking hot," said my assistant and best friend, Kim, looking at my screen. "You fanning yourself for a coffee burn or for this stud muffin?"

"Want to share why you're an hour late?" I'd long ago learned to expect Kim when I saw her. She never missed an appointment or meeting but believed her hours were completely flexible.

"I got the chance for a penis power hour, so I took it," she said, unfazed. "Anyway, go dry your top while I read this application."

"I'm going to pop to Ebony's downstairs and buy a new one. Screw it." Our office was situated above a boutique, on a block that housed a cafe and a pet grooming salon. It was a great mix of female business owners and we had a collective that met monthly, *Female Entrepreneurs do it with their colleagues*. I'd not had the heart to tell Jax from the cafe that it sounded all kinds of wrong. She was a sensitive soul and likely to close the cafe for a few days if upset, and no one needed a lack of coffee and cake. No one.

I walked down the back stairs, out to the rear of the property and through the front entrance of the shop. Ebony took one look at me and shook her head.

"I know. Kim made me spill my coffee down myself."

"Oh, honey," Ebony said in her cut-glass accent. "Kimmy did you a huge favour. That top needs a cremation. RIP to the shapeless v-neck."

I groaned. Ebony was always trying to give me a makeover, and I just liked to keep things simple. Truthfully, I wasn't a power suit kind of girl. I preferred to meet clients looking like someone they felt comfortable to chat with intimately. It was through getting to know them that I knew who to match them up with. I was amazing at my job and had one of the most successful dating agencies in England. The irony being that the only person I couldn't find an ideal date for was myself. Running through my own application there had so far been no one who had measured up as a fit for me. I was awkward and picky and destined to be on my own forever.

"Here we go. This is what we need you in, darling. It will highlight that red hair and pale skin." Ebony held up a black tight tank top with a red rose on the front. It had an overlay of black netting. It would go with the skinny jeans I was wearing, but goth girl really wasn't me. I was a jeans and plain tee wearing girl who on the rare occasion she got dressed up would wear floral tea dresses.

"Have you got something else, a little lighter in colour?" I asked.

"No, sorry, I have nothing else in your size."

I looked around the rest of the well-stocked boutique and raised an eyebrow.

Ebony exuded calm. "All of this stock is pre-ordered. You can only have the top you're holding."

I sighed and handed over my credit card and went into the changing rooms to change it over. Looking in the dressing room mirror I saw that Ebony was totally right. It really did suit my complexion. Maybe I should adopt a goth girl persona and start watching *The Corpse Bride* and wear black lipstick?

Ebony clapped her manicured hands complete with red talons when I emerged from the changing rooms. "Look at you. A vision. Can I curl your hair up a little before you leave?"

"No." I snapped. "Leave me alone, you're giving me a complex."

"Darling, you keep wondering why you're single and I'm trying to help you. He's coming you see. The one for you. We need you ready for him."

I raised an eyebrow again. "Ebony, are you pissed from last night still? How many voddies did you have? Or, do you have a bottle behind the counter again because I've told you, it will put customers off if you dance with them. How many times have we had this conversation now?"

Ebony's gaze darted towards the door, then she lowered her voice. "Look, I will confess all. I drink vodka at times because the thoughts become too much, too intense. If I'm a little mellow, I can cope and they dissipate. Otherwise I get bad migraines. Anyway, I've not had any alcohol today, but I'm receiving strong thoughts when you are around. That you must be prepared because your 'one' is coming."

I rubbed at my eyes. It was a day for lunatics. I needed to chat to Kim and Jax about keeping a close eye on Ebony because she seemed a little mentally fragile. It was a struggle to run a business on your own, and maybe she'd reached for the alcohol a few times too many. I decided the best thing to do was to purchase the top and let her do my hair.

She sat me on a stool at the counter and wound my long hair around tongs until I had the most beautiful spiral curls. I would never have taken the time to do this for myself. Ebony reached for some cosmetics that she had displayed under the counter and I was about to protest when her mouth set in a pout. I sighed and let her put makeup on me. I could always call down the corner shop on the next block for some baby wipes to take it off. In the meantime, three customers had come in and were watching Ebony at work. It turned into a makeup class. I felt like I was on freaking QVC.

"Voila. Go back to the changing rooms and see!"

I hopped off the stool and looked at myself in the mirror. I hardly recognised the person looking back. She'd put bronzer on my face and used the cosmetics to give me a healthy glow instead of my usual wan look.

"Okay," I come back out. "I admit defeat. You're amazing."

"I know." She smiled as she wrapped up makeup sets for the three women who were watching. "You need this." She holds up a fourth set. "So altogether that's fifty-three pounds eighty pence with your staff discount." She waved the credit card I'd handed over earlier and I nodded and watched as she rang me up. I was going to kill Kim. That coffee spill had set me back a small fortune.

I went back upstairs and stood in the doorway. Kim was still sitting in front of my computer.

"So, what do you need me to do..." She paused. "Holy, fuck, where's Shelley? Seriously, where's she gone? Who is this beautiful creature in front of me? I'm straight as they come but hell, I reckon I could be persuaded."

I crossed my arms. "Ebony decided I needed a makeover, and it's cost me the best part of sixty quid so don't expect a bonus this month."

"Hey." Kim waved her hands in the air. "I wasn't the one who got so flustered looking at Mr Hot Vampire that I spilled my drink down myself."

"Oh yes. That reminds me, can you contact him and send him a decline email?"

Kim looked down at the floor. "Oh, where's my earing gone?"

I gave her a pinched stare. "You don't have pierced ears, Kim. Sit up straight and look me in the eyes. What have you done?"

"Welllll..." She bit on her lip. "His photo is reaalllly hot, and I thought we didn't get too many sexy men coming in, so I sent him an appointment for the next stage."

"You did what?" I screamed. "He's obviously a complete nutcase. What if he really thinks he's a vampire and tries to bite one of us?"

"I don't think he would because he's an old vampyre, spelled the old-fashioned way. He must have got past that fledgling stage long ago."

"He's *not* a real vampire."

"I know, but since *True Blood* finished, I'm desperately missing Eric. Also, Ian Somerhalder got all married and loved up. Let's interview the hottie. We can just reject him when his true crazy comes out. I really don't think he'll try to bite us. Not if he wants us to find him a wife."

"Kim, could you, as my assistant, please get me

another coffee, and a chocolate doughnut. Things are stressful today. Now, what time have you arranged for Mr Landry to come for an interview?"

"I said eight pm, at Hanif's."

"Hanif's? The Indian restaurant?"

"Yes, it's dark. Mr Landry can't come out before then."

"Go get me my coffee. Do not forget the doughnut. In fact, make it two doughnuts. Go now."

"God, you're in a mood. Are you jealous cos I got some this morning?"

"A box of doughnuts. A box of twelve." I shouted after her swinging backside.

Chapter Two

Shelley

"So..." Kim tried to look innocent, gazing up through her dark fringe.

"Why aren't you looking ready?" I asked her. We'd been working up until we needed to set off for the date. She owed the hours due to her 'flexitime' working.

"So, I can't make it," she said. "I totally forgot I had a doctor's appointment booked for eight. Sorry I double-booked, but I'm sure you'll be okay with the vamp."

I sighed heavily. "Firstly, he is *not* a real vampire. Secondly, there are no doctors appointments happening after 5pm. It's England. They all go home for tea. So what the hell are you talking about?"

"I so do have an appointment." She pouted. "With Dr Francis Love. In his bedroom, at 8pm."

"Go." I made shooing motions at her with my hands. "I've heard enough of your nonsense today. I will deal with Mr Landry. You'd encourage his delusions anyway. I need to make sure he knows I'm not taking any bullshit."

"That's hurtful you know? Saying I talk nonsense. You're mean. A mean boss. I'll need to come in late tomorrow so I have time to work through my hurt feelings."

With that she gave me a wink and walked through the door, leaving me to grab my fake leather jacket and head to Hanif's.

∼

"Hey, Rav. I'm meeting a Mr Landry."

Rav, one of the waiters at Hanif's, had rushed over to greet me on my arrival.

"Yes, yes. He is here. He asked to be seated in the back corner. I will take you through to him."

I followed Rav to the back of the restaurant; the smell of delicious spices wafted up my nose and made my stomach rumble. I'd not had any lunch, having been stuffed full of chocolate doughnuts, and now my body was reminding me it needed sustenance. As Theodore turned to face me, another part of my body made its feelings known. Yeah, my vajayjay definitely needed sustenance. It had been a *long* time.

He was even more striking in the flesh. That dark hair and his dark, almost black looking irises contrasted against the paleness of his skin. I thought I was pale, but I think he even outdid me. I wondered if he was anaemic. He had a slight rosy glow to his cheeks, which might have been a little show of embarrassment or nervousness. Oh bless him. He stood up and held out his hand, towering over my five feet seven frame.

"Miss Linley?"

I held out my hand. "Mr Landry."

His hands were cold to the touch, rather like my feet when I got in bed at night. I felt myself tremble slightly, but that might have been due to him being majorly hot, rather than cold.

"Call me Theo, please."

"Okay, well I'm Shelley." Like I said, I preferred being down to earth with my clients. Now just to wait for this one to admit to pranking me and we could get on with finding him a match.

Rav came over to us. "Can I get you any drinks?"

"Erm, a glass of white wine for me, Rav, please." I rarely drank on the job but then again, I rarely interviewed a nutcase who thought he was a vampire.

"Small, or large?"

"The biggest you have."

"Two glasses and you get the bottle free?"

I sucked on my top lip and nodded, "Sold. Bring the bottle, my man."

"And for you, sir?"

"A glass of red please. Do you have a Merlot?"

"Yes, sir." He handed us a menu each. "I shall get your drinks and will be back to take your food order."

We nodded.

"So," Theo said. "What happens at this follow up interview?"

I placed a napkin over my lap, feeling edgy and like I needed to do something. "I go through the questionnaire with you. Ask any additional questions I may have and then if everything is in order, I run it through the computer programme back at the agency and see if we have some matches for you."

"And if you don't?"

"You can either stay on our books as new people join all the time, or you are of course free to try another agency."

"But there are no other agencies in Withernsea."

"Yes, but there are agencies around the country, the world even, and the internet is a big place. I'm sure you could find someone."

"I have more chance of finding a mate in Withernsea, this is where my kind live."

Here it was.

"Your kind, as in vampire?"

"Of course. What else could I mean?" He looked at me with a furrowed brow.

"Er, nothing. Let me get my paperwork out of my bag."

"After dinner," he said. "Let's enjoy the meal first and you can get to know me better."

Great. I had planned to go through the questionnaire, declare him unsuitable and hot tail it out of here. Although looking at the menu I could see they had prawn puri, my absolute favourite. Hey, hang on, vampires couldn't be near garlic, could they? That's what Kim said. So what would happen if I ordered a garlic and coriander naan bread? Hmmm. I decided to go along with his fantasy world and turn his prank against him.

Our drinks arrived and Rav got his notebook and pen ready.

"And for you, sir?"

I hated that. Why did they ask the guy what they wanted first? Totally sexist. Bastard.

"I will just have a chicken balti, with a plain naan bread. Thank you."

"No starter for you, sir?"

"No thank you. I'm afraid I already ate a little before I came."

I pulled a face. Who did that? Arranged a dinner and then ate already. Wanker.

"And for you, madam?"

I wanted a starter. I wanted prawn puri, but now dickwad wasn't having one, I wouldn't either. Otherwise I'd be here even longer than I needed to be.

I studied the menu sucking on my lip. "I will have

... let's see ... I'd like your Chef's special: the garlic chicken, and garlic and coriander naan bread."

Rav leaned over and whispered in my ear. "This is why you're single."

I gave him a dirty look. "This is a business dinner."

"Oh, okay then. Food coming right up." Rav scurried away.

"So, you say you ate already?" I asked him. "You might not want to arrange dinner with a woman if you've eaten beforehand."

"It was just my regular O-neg," he said. "Obviously without it, I'd die." He showed me his teeth. "Are they a little red stained? That's why I ordered a glass of red, it disguises the blood stains."

I sighed.

"Look, Theo, can we just drop this whole you're a vampire thing?"

"But I am a vampire."

"No, you're not. Vampires aren't real."

"I am." He sat up straight. "How old are you?"

I folded my arms across my chest. "Not that it's any of your business but I'm twenty-six."

"Well I'm one hundred years your senior, so in this circumstance, I'm afraid you need to have some respect and believe me when I tell you that I am a vampire."

I was about to get up and leave but Rav brought over a pickle tray and some poppadoms and I was weak.

"Fine, you're a vampire."

Theo breathed out a sigh of relief. "Usually at this point the woman leaves. Admit it. If you were a date, you would have left by now."

"If I wasn't hungry, I would have left." I bit into a poppadom. "You might have to not tell people at first, maybe? So that they get to know you as a person before you confess your secret?"

"Hmmm. I don't know."

I met his cool gaze. "Look, let's practice tonight. While we eat dinner, pretend you're not a vampire, but a regular human guy." I pointed. "Like Rav, a regular guy like Rav."

"Rav is not a regular guy. Rav is a demon," Theo replied. A crease appeared between his eyebrows. "How long have you lived in Withernsea? You are not very aware of your surroundings. I was told the people of Withernsea were like the undead. That's why I stayed here."

It was one thing to insult me. It was quite another to insult my hometown.

"Hey. Just because we're a quiet seaside town does not mean you get to diss the people that live here."

Theo turned to me and started to chuckle.

"Do you know I have to take regular classes to keep up to date with modern technology and language? I only learned diss in 2015. By the way, I very much like your outfit. You look dazzling, simply sensational."

"Pardon?" I was still trying to catch up with the nonsense spouting from his mouth.

"I'm pretending to be a human male, so I'm complimenting your outfit."

My jaw set. "Oh. You don't actually like it then? You're saying that because it's expected of a human male?"

"Well, I preferred the attire of my day, when you could catch a glimpse of a lady's bare ankle and think all your birthdays had come at once. Your outfit is quite acceptable though. The trousers are a little tight, but this is compensated by the flow of the top over your bottom. It clings over your breasts a little. Always remember, less is more. It creates lust in a man."

"Are you quite finished?" I was gripping my knife so hard my knuckles had turned white.

"Yes, these Indian starters aren't for me. I'm saving myself for my main course."

Would it have been considered rude if I punched a potential client in the throat?

"Why do you think you haven't already found the woman of your dreams? Do you think it might be your way with words?" I huffed.

His eyes dropped to the floor and his mouth downturned. "I don't know how to approach a woman anymore. Once upon a time they wanted you to take charge. Now they want to be equal. My head's all over the place with how to approach a date. I've had over one thousand girlfriends. I'm very jaded about the whole thing."

One thousand girlfriends? He needed to be on *The Bachelor,* not the books of my dating agency. Okay, if he'd not found a wife in over one thousand girlfriends there was definitely something wrong with him – something more than him believing he was a vampire. Surely, there'd be at least one Withernsea woman desperate enough to overlook the fantasist behaviour and take Theo home to bed every night?

The smell of garlic permeated the air as our main courses were brought to the table. Theo didn't flinch. I waited until Rav had left and tore off a piece of garlic naan. I threw it at his face to see if he had a reaction.

He reared back in his seat. "What are you doing?" Hmmm, a little reaction. Not sure the garlic touched him though. I took my fork and flicked some of my garlic chicken sauce at his hands. Once again, he leapt back, shaking his fingers. He picked up the water jug from our table and poured some over his hand.

Rav ran over. "Is everything okay?"

"Is it Indian culture to throw food at your friend while they eat?" Theo asked.

Rav turned to me and I looked away.

"Shelley?"

"I'm sorry, I have a small twitch." I punched out my arm and wiggled it around. "Must have been a trapped nerve. It seems to be okay now."

Rav leaned over again "This is why you're sin-"

"I get it," I snapped. "Tomorrow, I'll book in for *The Undateables* and appear on TV, okay?"

"What is this *Undateables*?" Theo asked. "I don't watch much TV. Just the news and *Celebs Go Dancing*."

We took our seats again. Theo wiping his hands on his table napkin.

"*Celebs Go Dancing?*"

"Yes, I love watching the old-style dances and of course you have to support your own."

I take a deep breath. "Go on."

"Sophia is one of us. Can you not tell, with all that dark hair and eyeliner, plus the fact she never appears to age?"

"Sophia Coleman is a vampire?" I clarified.

"Yes. She bit Ken. That's the real reason he retired as Head Judge last year."

Help me God. Help me now. If the chicken hadn't tasted so damn fine, I would have run for the hills. That and the fact that Theo was *so* pleasing on the eye. Jeez, I was that desperate for a bit of eye candy, I'd risk my life having a meal with a psychopath. I made a note to pick up an *Undateables* application form. They'd probably snap my hand off. A dating agency owner who could find love for everyone else but was all alone.

I began to feel guilty about the garlic incident. "Sorry about the food. Pass me your hand, let me check I didn't harm you."

Theo wiggled his wrist at me. "No harm done."

"Ha. I knew you weren't a vampire," I spat.

"Pardon?"

"Garlic. It was a test. I touched you with garlic. You should have burned or something."

Theo sat back in his seat, his eyes wide.

"That is folklore. Vampires do not react to garlic. But it concerns me that in order to check this fact you threw not one, but two items of garlic containing foodstuffs at me, knowing that the potential was there for me to burn. You would wish me harm? I have done nothing to deserve it."

Theo pushed his chair further back. "I made a mistake coming here. I'm not sure I'm altogether safe in your company. You seem a little, well, insane." He took his wallet out of his jacket pocket.

Vampire dude thought *I* was insane. Well there was an outcome I wasn't expecting.

"Theo, I'm sorry. I didn't really think it would do anything."

"Then why try?"

"I just wanted to show you that you weren't a vampire."

Theo stared at me. "I see."

He insisted on paying the bill and escorted me outside. There was no one else around, but the number 46 bus was due on the half hour, so I intended to make my way to the bus stop around the corner.

"Would you like a lift home?" he offered. "You would have to make a vow to not try to cause me harm."

"No, it's fine. I'm sorry about the food throwing thing. It wasn't very professional of me. Maybe you could call into the office tomorrow afternoon and I'll go through your application with you then?"

"Do you have an appointment around five?"

Of course. He needed vampire hours. What was it about him that prevented me from telling him to get lost? It was like he had an allure. Yeah, Shelley. More like you have horny hormones. I was due on at any moment and always felt like I could mount my bedposts when I was like this.

In fact, was that a tell-tale trickle I felt? Well, that was a fitting end to this awkward evening; time to go to bed with a hot water bottle.

"Aaarrrgh."

I turned to see what was the matter with Theo, perhaps he had a weak stomach for Indian spices? I froze in place—stunned—as right in front of me two fangs descended and his eyes went red.

"Aaarghhhhhhhhhh. You're a vampire." I screamed, turning on my heel and running as fast as I could towards the bus stop where I could see the number 46 in the distance.

Theo ran after me, catching up to me with lightning, unnatural speed. Before I knew it, he put me in his arms and ran with me. In what seemed like five seconds I was outside my door, trying my best to not vomit up my garlic chicken.

"What, the-?"

"What, the?" I repeated.

But when I turned around Theo was gone.

Chapter Three

Shelley

I unlocked the door of my two-bedroomed semi-detached home and staggered through to the sofa where I sprawled out. What the hell had just happened?

It was the wine; I had drunk most of a bottle. Or, *Theo had spiked it!*

But that made little sense because he'd brought me home and left me. Surely the point of spiking my drink would be to take advantage of me?

Hey, how did he know where I lived? *OMG. Theo was a stalker!*

But that made no sense either because if he was a stalker, he would have been hanging around here and work, wouldn't he? Not meeting me in restaurants where everyone could see him.

There was no way he had fangs and red eyes.

I decided I must have fallen asleep on the sofa after

meeting him. That would be it. I went out, had too much wine, Theo brought me to the door and then I'd had a bad dream. Seemed I need to stop watching *Lucifer* on TV before going to bed.

I rolled onto my back and stared at the ceiling. Right now, I didn't feel the slightest bit drunk. In fact, I felt perfectly okay, except for thoughts of the weirdness of the evening out. I replayed what I'd seen in my mind.

Canines descending.

Eyes going red.

No fucking way. He must have put something in my drink. He'd got to have. I was having delusions.

I got his questionnaire out of my bag. It was only a quarter to eleven and in any case, if he was a vampire he'd be up all night, right?

I got his number from the papers and dialled him on my mobile.

"Hello?"

"Theo. It's Shelley."

"Shelley. Oh thank goodness you called. I thought it best I leave you but I wasn't sure if I was doing the right thing. Are you okay? Are you in shock? Perhaps you could get yourself a cup of tea with a few sugars."

"Theo. I'm going to come right out and say it. Did you spike my drink because I've had some weird hallucinations tonight?"

"Ah."

"Ah...? Do you mean you did?"

"No." He sighed. "I mean ah, you've done what everyone else does – enter into the stages of supernatural denial. 'Oh, there must be some logical explanation. I didn't really see his fangs and a flash of a red eye or two'. No, far more reasonable to suggest to the nice gentleman who took me for dinner that he drugged me."

I sighed. "There's no other explanation."

"Other than the fact I'm a vampire."

"I don't think I can help you find a date or a wife, Theo, you're not mentally stable."

"You threw naan bread and curry at me to see if the garlic burned and now you're accusing me of being a sicko who spiked your drink. Which one of us sounds like a lunatic?"

Damn. The twat had a point.

"The problem is that I've never met a supernatural person before and well, I just don't believe in it. There has to be a logical explanation, like for instance your family have dental issues and there's some weird genetic defect that makes your eyes look a funny colour, probably in a certain light."

"Or, it could be that my vampire nose detected the sweet smell of blood coming from between your thighs and because it took me by surprise and my guard was down, your sweet perfume made my fangs descend."

"Ugh. That's the sickest thing I ever heard. Menstruation is not sexy."

"I didn't say it was. What I said, was the smell appealed to my vampire nature. I don't and won't ever drink that. It's not pure."

"And that's the end of that conversation. I don't know why I called. Why I expected anything you said to make any sense."

"Yet you did call. Because one small part of you, Shelley, one small part deep inside you, wonders if I am telling the truth."

I sat back against the sofa. Did I want this to be the truth? Maybe so. Maybe it would provide some excitement in my boring life. Yes, I had good friends here, but I didn't have family around. I was adopted, and had never gotten along with my adoptive parents, not after they had a child naturally ten months later and made sure I knew that I wouldn't have been adopted had that pregnancy test showed positive earlier than it did. Oh well, I was a career woman, I decided. I didn't need a social life, or a man. Instead I'd carry on matchmaking for everyone else.

"Are you still there?"

Shit, I'd gone off into one of my 'fuck you all, I don't need anyone' daydreams. Actually, if it was at night, shouldn't it be called a nightdream?

"Look, Shelley, I'm going to Facetime you, and slowly show you my fangs again and this time you have to try not to freak out. Although you probably will. It usually takes a person three viewings before they believe they're real. The third time they always want to touch them, like I'd want someone's dirty fingers in my mouth."

"A vampire who sucks people's blood can't deal with dirty fingers?" I scoffed.

"Hygiene is everything. For years now my blood has been delivered. It's a long time since I had a woman who let me partake directly from the source."

"So you don't grab people from the street and drain them dry?"

"No, and I don't sparkle either. Any more stereotypical questions in that head of yours?"

"You'd better Facetime me first."

The call came through. I accepted and there he was on the screen. My core went slick at the sight of him. Traitorous hussy.

"Are you ready?" he asked.

Oh God, yeeeaaass, came from the inner workings of my mind which was no doubt colluding with said traitorous hussy core. Instead I went with a simple, "Yes."

He looked into the camera and opened his mouth to show a row of perfectly normal teeth.

I was disappointed.

He caught my expression. "Hold on there a second, Shelley. I can't just perform like that. I'm not a circus animal. Now let me get a drink." He held a glass of what looked like tomato juice up to the camera, but I got a feeling it wasn't tomato juice at all. I watched with morbid fascination as his fangs descended.

"Oh my God."

I slapped my hand over my mouth, careful not to drop the phone. "I'm sorry, blaspheming affects you, doesn't it?"

"Here we go again. Let's go over everything you think about vampires."

"Okay. So, you can hear the word God, etc."

"Yes, and I can say holy crap or anything like that."

"Can you go into a church?"

"I hope so, cos I kind of want to get married, remember? Although I'd have to use a fake ID as they never believe I'm 126. I do look fantastic for my age."

"Can a stake kill you?"

"Clarify. What sort? Steak meat or stake, stabby thing?"

"A stabby thing."

"No, another piece of misinformation. It's steak that can kill us. We have sensitive throats. It often gets stuck there and chokes my kind to death."

"And garlic has no effect?"

"No, unless it's in a fresh from the oven sauce and burns your skin."

I bit my lip. "Uhhmm, sorry about that."

"Just promise not to throw food at me again. Going forward."

"Going forward?"

"I'm seeing you again at five tomorrow. Do I need to wear protective armour?"

I laughed. "No. You'll be safe. From me at least."

His fangs ascended, and he frowned. "Who might I not be safe from?"

"All the other women near where I work. You're not exactly ugly."

"I used to model you know?"

"You did?"

"Yeah, kept getting mobbed everywhere I went so had to fake my own death. That was Los Angeles in the 1950's."

"I can't get my head one hundred percent around you being a vampire. Never mind that you would have lived a massively long life and have done and know so many things."

"I have lots of experience," he said, and he goddamn smirked.

Down girl, I told my pussy, and no I didn't have a cat. *Don't let your mind go there. Don't let your mind go there.*

How many women has he slept with?

Can he have normal sex?

Does he only have one penis? What if vampires had two? Oh my word, the possibilities...

"You've gone into a daydream again. I guess I'd better let you get some sleep," he said.

"Yes, sleep. So, you won't be sleeping yet?"

"No. I go to my room around 6am and then I'll get up around 4pm. The whole sunlight thing is a crock of shit too. I don't get badly burned. It's just that our body clocks are set for that time and to go against it can make us feel very ill."

"So, dating wise you can only see a woman from 4pm to 6am?"

"Unless they come to my room. Although it wouldn't be much fun for them as I'm dead to the world then. Or of course, if they're a vampire themselves they could sleep with me, but that would only happen if things got serious."

"And do you sleep in a coffin?"

At this he guffaws. "No, I don't sleep in a coffin. I sleep in a perfectly normal, though King-sized bed, given my height. It has a lovely memory foam mattress. I do however, have top security in the room and lock myself in with windows and shutters. I'm vulnerable when I'm asleep."

"What, someone might break in and stuff some pieces of steak down your throat?"

"Stranger things have happened to try to kill us in the past." His expression became subdued.

"So, how can you die?"

"There's a place we can go. You're counselled and then if they agree with your decision to end your life, you say a secret incantation and you crumble to dust."

"But can people kill you?"

"Why, was throwing naan bread not entertaining enough for you?"

I laughed.

"We can be killed but I'm not going to say how. The less people that know the better. No disrespect, but I barely know you."

"I understand."

"Time for bed now, Shelley."

Oh my God, would he stop saying things like that? He had a low, growly voice that made it sound like a command.

I yawned. "Yes, time to call it a night. Thank you for showing me your fangs."

"Do you believe me?" he asked, looking at me with a hint of vulnerability in his eyes.

"Right now, I believe you. In the morning when the wine has left my system and my rational mind has had time to dissuade me from the evidence, then I'll probably need to put my filthy hands in your mouth."

"Well, seeing as it's you." He winked.

I ended the call and made my way up to my room. My lovely double bed, just for me. An advantage of living alone. My mind conjured up an image of a six-foot-two-inch hunk laid there with his feet hanging off the edge. I shook my head to make the vision go away.

"Enough already," I whispered. "We somehow have to find him a wife."

I visited the bathroom then quickly undressed, put on my pjs and then dived under the duvet. Sleep claimed me in minutes.

~

"Shelley."

I sat up in bed. Who shouted?

A woman with long dark hair with a white streak running through it sat in a golden chair at the end of my bed.

But I didn't have a golden chair? And it was like, glowing.

"Shelley. Can you hear me?"

"Who are you?"

The woman clapped her hands. "Oh my God, can you hear and see me? At last! The curse is broken. You believe!"

"Who are you? What the hell are you talking about?"

"Sssh. Don't say hell. She doesn't like people using it to curse."

"Who doesn't?"

"Lucy."

"This is the strangest dream I've ever had. Now if you'll excuse me, I've had a mindfucking night already having potentially met a vampire and so if my mind could let me have a restful night's sleep it would be much appreciated."

"This isn't a dream. I'm in your dream because I'm not on your plane, but I'm really here."

"Yeah? And who are you?"

She looked sad. "I'm your mother."

I bolted upright, sweat pouring from my forehead. Stupid dream. Meeting Theo had messed with my head. I was probably going to need therapy or something. Oh God, what if he was a figment of my imagination as well? Maybe I had gone well and truly insane. I picked up my phone to see what time it was and noticed I had a new message, sent thirty minutes before.

Theo: Just in case you wake up and wonder if it was all a dream...

Underneath was a photo of his fangs.

I was too tired to give it any more thought. I fell back to sleep and this time I didn't have strange dreams about the supernatural or my parents.

Chapter Four

Shelley

A miracle had occurred. When I'd got to work Kim was already there, waiting, with a paper cup full of dark, delicious coffee on my desk and one in her hand.

"All messages taken care of. So, all you have to do is take a seat and tell me about Mr Dark and Delicious."

Ah, she had an agenda. Figured. Couldn't usually rouse her out of bed before 9:30am.

I slumped into the seat behind my desk and yawned.

Kim gasped. "Oh my God. Did you stay out all night? Was it love at first bite?"

I rolled my eyes. "Can you lower your voice, just a teeny tiny bit, only it's too early for diva operatics."

"God, what bit your arse, or rather did he not and you're disappointed this morning?"

I rubbed at my face. "I didn't sleep well. I had

nightmares. Now, let me have a drink of my coffee and I'll update you."

Kim clapped her hands.

"I want deets. Every single detail of the evening." She winked.

I sighed and took several large gulps of my drink.

"Okay, so write this down." I indicated for Kim to pick up her pen and notepad.

"I. Am. A. Nosy. Bitch."

"Hahahaha." Kim tilted her head. "So, meal last night. What happened?"

"Well, basically it would appear that he is a vampire, but he has no aversion to garlic, which I found out when I threw some naan bread at him."

I recounted the details of the meal and Kim shook her head. "Oh my God, Shelley, I'm surprised we don't have a lawsuit on our hands this morning. You attacked a potential customer."

I stared at her. "That's all you have to say on the matter? Nothing about the fact he's a vampire?"

"Oh, if he wants to think he's one of the undead, as long as it doesn't hurt anyone, what's the harm? Might be a nice little kink for a boyfriend to have, actually. My neck's quite an erogenous zone, a few little nips would be nice."

"No. He *is* a vampire. He showed me his fangs."

Kim huffed. "You're being very silly this morning, Shelley. So, are we taking him on our books?"

"He's coming in at five. I didn't get a chance to go through the questionnaire."

"Why not?"

"Because I was too busy trying to get him to admit to not being a vampire."

"Oh, Shelley." Kim tutted and once again shook her head. "We do very well at this agency, but there's always room for growth. So he wants to live his life as a vampire. Where's the harm as long as he doesn't try to drain someone of their blood? There were three people living their lives as mermaids the other day on *This Morning*. They'd even done a course. One was a merman."

"Well, prepare to be here until six, because we're going through the questionnaire together. I want you to meet him and see what you think. I want a second opinion."

"Stay behind to stare at a hottie for an hour. Gee, I'm not sure I can fit that in. What time's he coming again? Phwoar o'clock?"

"Five."

"I couldn't think of anything that went with five." Kim pouted, her dark fringe falling in her eyes.

"So, how was your evening, anyway? With the love doctor."

A dreamy look settled on her face. "Oh, it was amazing. You see, he has a kink. He likes me to pretend

I'm dead. I lay on the bed all corpse like and he reanimates me with his magic wand." She winked.

I made a retching noise and pretended to heave. "Jesus Christ, Kim. That's not normal."

"You need to get laid. I bet you've only ever done the missionary position. You'd have to lie really flat on your back with that stick stuck up your arse."

"I'm not going to respond to that."

"Cos it's true. I'm going to quiz old True Blood to see if he'd like to take a bite out of you."

"You'll stick to the questionnaire and behave yourself. I'm not part of the system as you well know. How unprofessional would it be to put myself in the algorithm?"

"Shut up. Put yourself in when you get a spare five minutes. I do. It's just I have so many dates I don't need to use the info. Who matches up with you, show me. We've got time."

"No."

"God, you're no fun today at all."

I looked at the floor.

"Oh my God. Does *no one* match up with you? Is that it? You're far too choosy, Shelley. If you don't change you're going to be alone forever and your fanny is going to heal up."

I place my hands over my ears.

"You can go to your office now. Go deal with the new clients. My ears are bleeding."

She left and I welcomed the silence. I fired up my laptop. Four new applications had come in since Kim had been in here.

I heard her door bang, and she rushed into my office. "Have you seen the new applications?"

"I've only just put my laptop on, Kim. You've only been out of the office four minutes."

"Well, it seems that True Blood is recommending you to his mates," she said, her eyes going wide as she smiled.

"You need to stop calling him that. His name is Theo."

"Anyway, open the first email." She beckoned for me to get a move on.

Name: Darius Wild
Supporting information: Wolf shifter (also known as werewolf)

Name:Dominic Moore
Supporting information:Demon

Name:Isaac Renshaw
Supporting information:shifter (bear)

I didn't bother to open the last one, scared of what I would find. Either someone was having a rather large laugh at my expense, or Withernsea, and indeed the world around me, weren't what I thought they were.

"See, True Blood's obviously told his kinky friends about us. He's good for business," Kim said. "We just need to hope that the women of Withernsea are up for some role play!"

I immersed myself in work and debated whether I believed Theo to be a vampire. I went back to thinking he was a magician or a theatre prop person. The fang trick was obviously very clever makeup. Fancy me believing he was a real-life vampire! I really needed to quit watching *Twilight* repeats just to ogle Jasper.

Kim brought the post through. On the top lay a bright red envelope with my name written in a swirly font. "I've not opened that one cos it looks like a personal invitation."

"Thank you," I told her and put the post on my desk.

"Aren't you going to open it?"

I folded my arms across my chest. "So you've not opened it for my privacy but you want me to open it while you're here so you can see what it is?"

"Well, duh?" She took a seat.

Give me strength.

I opened the envelope and took out the card

within. A large, dead spider fell out, and I screamed and pushed my chair back.

"Oh my fucking God. Who would do that?"

"It's almost Halloween. It's obviously a fake spider and a Halloween party invite. For God's sake I'll read it, you're hopeless," she said, grabbing the card.

As she read it, the blood drained from her face.

"What is it?" I asked.

She passed the card to me. Inside it read:

Stay away from things that don't concern you in Withernsea. We were all okay as we were. Refuse to help Theo or you may find yourself dead either way.

"It's a death threat! You need to call the police," yelled Kim.

"Don't be stupid. It's obviously a prank. Either that or a patient from the psychiatric hospital Theo, no doubt, was an in-patient at, has escaped. I'll be extra vigilant but I'm sure it's nothing. I'm not going to take Theo on the books anyway, so no harm done."

"Well, I'm bringing a rounders bat into the office from now on and we all know the only sports I do are water ones." Kim huffed and turned to leave. "If we get any more threats, I'm phoning the police, and that's the end of it."

"Fine." I held my hands up. "If there are any more, we'll phone the cops. Jeez."

Theo arrived promptly at 5pm and Kim introduced herself and indicated he should take a seat opposite me. I remained behind my desk, but Kim decided to seat herself next to him. He moved his chair about a foot away from her and she scowled.

"Sorry," he said. "You smell a little of magic and I find it overpowering. It gives me a headache."

"Oh, I'm wearing Miss Dior, actually," Kim said haughtily. "Magic must be a knock-off version. I'm not into copies, I like originals."

He looked back at her strangely and then at me. I shook my head at him and mimed the word 'no'. He shrugged and sat back in his chair.

"Okay. So, first of all, would you like a drink?" I asked him.

"No, I had some refreshment before I came here," he said, and I noted the slight pink tinge to his cheek. Oh-kay then.

"You smell as well," Kim said. "Like you've been around pigs or something." She turned her nose up.

"I called at a local farm for my refreshment today. My apologies," he said to her.

"Right, well, if we could get on with going over these questions." I tapped into my screen. "Okay, so I might have to change a few of these answers, with your consent, of course, just to make the algorithm work better."

"Whatever you feel necessary. As long as ultimately, I find a wife, I have no objections."

"So, your full name is Theodore Robert Landry and your date of birth 1 January 1891, making you 126."

"That is correct."

"Well, my system won't work with anyone over the age of 100, so I'll change that to 1 January 1981, making you 36, which is an optimum age.

"There's nothing I need to change about your appearance." I looked over the section.

Kim snorted.

"What is it, Kim?" I asked, starting to wish I'd not asked her to sit in.

"No disrespect, Theo, but you look like you've not seen sunlight in decades."

"I haven't."

"Look, it might go with the whole, 'I'm a vampire' thing, but it's going to put women off. You need a nice glow. Shelley, give me that makeup palette you bought."

"No!"

Theo raised his hand. "Actually, if it can make me look healthier, I wouldn't mind trying it."

I ran my hands through my hair while Kim helped herself to the palette from my handbag. Maybe I should make an appointment to see the GP tomorrow and get some psychiatric pills for delusions, and opiates for my nerves. Because it did appear that my assistant was giving a vampire a makeover in front of me.

She held the mirror part of the palette up to him and he moved his head from side to side as he stared in it. "Oh my goodness, this is amazing. Where can I get one of these? I need to purchase one immediately I leave here."

"I thought vampires didn't have reflections?" I asked.

"Stereotyping still?" He shot back.

"The palettes are from Ebony's downstairs. Have you got thirty quid? I'll go fetch you one."

He took the money from his wallet, gave it to her and sat back in his chair. "This is going to transform my life," he said. "Could I just put this palette on my Instagram while we wait for Kim to come back?"

I shrugged my shoulders. "Sure, why not? Maybe tweet it too."

"Oh, my kind don't do Twitter. We're far too wordy. Can't possibly say everything we want to divulge in less than 140 characters. Entirely impossible." He held up the palette. "Take this for example. I need to describe the feel, the tones, the wonderful packaging, where it's from, how best to apply."

"Okay, I get the picture," I said, just as Kim returned to the room.

"Okay, Boss. Carry on," she said.

"So, you mention in your application that you used

to live on a farm but now live on Sea View Road. However, you mention some trouble with the police calling round to see you?"

Theo sighed. "I want my birthplace back. I was happy there, and it's possible that the spirits of my family might hang around there, what with them having such traumatic deaths."

"When you drained them of their blood?" I clarified.

"It happens a lot with the first thirst. My sire should have protected me, but my father had been eating a juicy rare steak when he broke in."

"Let me guess, your sire choked?"

"He did. Leaving me alone and unfortunately meaning my family were no more. I didn't know then that I could have fed from at least one of them and brought them back to life."

"Wow, you are really great at this vamp shit." Kim pushed his arm. "You ever thought about being an actor? I reckon you'd win awards."

"I did that from 1926 to 1930," Theo said. "Learning lines gets boring after a while."

"You are such a hoot. Isn't he a laugh, Shelley?"

I raised my eyebrows. "He's something."

"Okay, Theo. So my suggestion while we try to find you a wife is for you to step back from your ongoing pursuit of the farm." Theo looked ready to protest, so I raised my hand. "Just until we get you a wife and then you could tell her about the farm. I mean, she might not want to live on one and then all your efforts would be for nothing. She might like a simple two-up, two-down with central heating and a patio."

"Fine. I suppose I could desist for a few weeks." Theo huffed.

"Now, Kim is going to go through our additional questionnaire which is all about your ideal woman and your dating habits."

"Okay," Kim said, crossing one leg over the other and trying to look official. "Do you have any preference for an age range, hair colour, any other personal details?"

"A fellow vampire would be excellent, or a woman willing to be changed." He looked at me. "I noted this on my first application."

"You could have changed your mind between then and now. Carry on, Kim."

"Okay. So someone who likes your vampire kink thing or who is willing to join in. Noted. Next question, when was the last date you went on? Describe it for us a little."

"It was a month ago. I met a nice lady in a bookshop and arranged to take her out for dinner. She ran out of the restaurant about a minute after we sat down."

"Why was that?" said Kim.

"Well, I've been looking for a wife for a long time

now and the whole dating, getting to know someone thing gets very tedious when after a month or two you tell them you're a vampire and they run away. I decided to get it out there at the beginning. Save wasting both of our time."

"And have you had dates with others of your kind? Surely there are places to meet other 'vampire' women."

"Yes. I've done that. But most vampire women are very jaded. If they're my age, they tend to have been married several times and for some reason prefer to spend the rest of the time single. They hang around university gyms in an evening, or student nights out where they take advantage of young men who are inebriated and don't remember anything the next day. Of course, the bite marks heal quickly, and the men put their tiredness down to an amazing night out, not a lack of iron."

I could tell by Kim's face that she believed he was a total fruit loop.

"Okay, well, if I could just have a word with Shelley outside, and then we'll be back to give you our decision." She told him, smiling afterwards though it didn't reach her eyes.

He nodded.

As soon as we were out of the door, she beckoned me to her office. "Beautiful guy. *If* you can find a woman who doesn't mind dating someone with a psychiatric disorder, you're golden. I think we're going to have to let him down."

"It's okay. I have a default in the programme that can come up with no matches. I've not had to use it before, but it means we can put him 'on hold', let him down without destroying his confidence. Essentially, we'll lead him to believe it's our fault we can't find any matches."

"Oh, what a great idea."

The truth was I couldn't match him up with any of my clients because for one, they'd assume, like Kim, that he was mental and secondly, I didn't know him well enough to know he wouldn't kill one of them. What if he got this thirst again that had made him drain his family members?

"Okay, let's go back," I told her and we retook our places in my office.

"Right, Theo. If you'd just give me a moment. I'll input the rest of your information and we'll see if we have any matches for you. If we do, then Kim can take your first month's membership payment, and we can get your first date arranged."

"That would be wonderful," he said. "May I watch it do its thing?"

"Of course. Just a minute."

I keyed in the information so it looked genuine and then pressed the button that would give him no matches before turning it around showing the 'search' procedure. Theo clapped. "Oh, my goodness. I didn't for a moment think this would be possible. I thought it might go against some ethics, but I'm very happy with this. Yes, I think your computer is amazing."

Wow, one satisfied customer. I span the screen back around to myself and then gasped, my mouth hanging open. I went through what I'd keyed in, running the process through my mind. Hell, I'd done everything right? So why was it showing Theo that his ideal partner was me?

CHAPTER Five

Theo

Some things were best left unsaid. I'd given away some vampire secrets, but I didn't get to live to 126 without keeping a lot of them to myself. For instance, the stake. It could absolutely kill me and reduce me to dust if it went through my heart. That was entirely true. Choking on steak? Well, it had happened to an old vampire friend on a night out. It hadn't killed him but put him off eating human food. I'd found my sire in a pile of ashes, killed by my father's farmhand.

Also, I had above average hearing, meaning that I could hear every word of the conversation between Shelley and Kim when they went to the other office.

But my best kept secret? I adored all things computers. At home I developed programmes for other vampires on how to keep track of our mortal enemies. I'd also developed a kind of Facebook for vampires called Faceblood. Years of experience and time on my hands allowed me to hack the weak to me security (quite adequate for others without my skills) and changed Shelley's system to show her as my ideal date.

Because I wanted her.

Since the minute I'd set eyes on her in that restaurant I'd decided no other woman would do.

She had hidden depths and secrets either she was unaware of or didn't wish to divulge. I could smell them on her.

More than that she was beautiful inside and out.

Setting up a dating agency, finding love for others when she didn't have it herself, was such a self-sacrificing thing to do. I'd looked up her history, seen that she'd been raised by adoptive parents, and as far as I could see she had no idea of her family background. Interesting.

Research into her agency showed that it was one of the best in England. I thought she deserved it to be the best, so I'd advertised her service on Faceblood. Hopefully she'd get some extra business. Dating a supernatural guy or girl was difficult, and there were a lot of us that remained single. We needed someone like Shelley on our side.

Shelley was still staring at the screen, but her colleague found the entire thing hilarious and couldn't stop laughing. "Well, Shelley, looks like you have a date. About time," she said. "Hey." She poked me in the arm. "I just thought, you coming here, we had an 'interview with the vampire', get it?"

I smiled at her. "Very witty. Do you know the whereabouts of all your main clients? Don't have any 'Lost Boys'."

"I can't go on a date with you," Shelley insisted. "It's against my ethics."

"I won't tell if you won't," said Kim.

"Not helping," Shelley replied.

"Well, technically, as you stated earlier until I pay for a month's membership I'm not actually a client. So, my apologies but I won't be joining your dating agency." I looked at Kim who beamed and gave me a thumbs up. I was warming to her even if she did smell. At some point, I'd have to warn her about sleeping with wizards. It could get messy.

"So, what say you, Shelley Linley? Would you like to go out with me? Preferably somewhere where there's no food you can throw?"

Shelley closed her eyes for a good thirty seconds. Then she opened them and nodded. "Why not? If nothing else I can teach you how to date a woman without scaring them away, and Christ knows I've nothing better to do with my evenings."

Well, it wasn't a no, but I can't say her acceptance did a lot for my diminished ego.

"Excellent. I'll pick you up from your apartment at 8pm tomorrow evening.

"I'll see you then, Theo," she replied.

I bowed to her and Kim and left the agency with a twinkle in my eye and a spring in my step. Things were looking up.

As I walked through the park on my way home, a stray firework hit a tree branch above me. It broke off, narrowly missing my head and landed on the ground in front of me, its broken point sticking up. Wow, if that had fallen a couple of seconds earlier and I'd tripped, that would have been the end of me. It really was my lucky day. I started singing Kylie's 'I should be so lucky'. God, I missed Scott and Charlene, they had the most epic romance. I'd really like to find that for myself.

Thursday night was cards night at mine. I arranged some dips, chips, and beer around the table and awaited my guests. Before long Rav, Darius, and my best friend Reuben—another vampire—were seated, and the cards had been dealt.

"It's going to be a lot better without Frankie here," said Darius.

"Yes. Despite his assurances that he wouldn't bewitch the cards, he won every hand until I threatened to drain him," Reuben commented with a glint in his eyes.

I looked at my friends in turn. I couldn't have him in the house again. "He smelled terrible. There isn't an odour remover that deals with removing the smell of magic."

"It has a smell?" said Rav. "I didn't smell anything."

"I've a very sensitive nose. He smells like rotten vegetables." I turned up my lip. "Anyway, we need to keep an eye on him. He's sleeping with the assistant at the dating agency. I smell a rat."

"That's not a nice way to describe him, even if he does stink like refuse to you," added Darius.

"I don't trust him. He's up to something, and if I can manage to get near enough without wanting to hurl, I'm going to find out what it is."

"I applied to the agency myself today," said Darius. "How are you getting on?"

I smiled. "I have my first date, and I'm very confident that eventually, she shall become my betrothed."

"Really?" Darius said. "That fast. Wow, I hope she can set me up that quickly."

"Alas, I think you may have to wait for her to accept that our kind really exist. She's currently on the fence —one moment she believes me and the next she's back to thinking it's parlour tricks."

"Well, it's not as difficult for me to disguise myself. As long as I don't have a date on the night of a full moon, I just come across as ripped and hairy. I hear human women are all about the man bun and beard at the moment." Darius added.

"Indeed, if their current book covers are anything to go by. There's quite a bit of shifter paranormal romance out there too, so you could be making dreams come true by dating human women."

"God, that would be epic."

"No." I shook my head. "It's not epic these days, it's sick. That's the current word for it."

"You just said 'alas'," Darius protested.

"So who's the date with?" Rav asked. "By the way, you owe me for calling you sir all night at Hanif's and pretending not to know you. At least you don't have to repeat the crazy that is Shelley. She runs that agency and is brilliant at matching others, but she has no clue about love. None." He turned to the others. "She threw hot food at Theodore yesterday. I don't know what her problem is. She's fit." Rav mimed a decent rack and patting a tush with his hands, "but completely insane."

He turned back to me. "So, who did she set you up with?"

"My date is with Shelley."

"What? You're crazy, and how? She's not in her own system, surely?"

"I rigged it when they went out of the room. I didn't have to pay either because it's not ethical so win-win."

"And she agreed to go out with you? A vampire? I told you she's crazy."

"There's something about her. A connection between us. She's mine, meant to be. I just know it."

"So you got a date without even paying?" Darius sulked. "We need to get rid of that wizard so I can have a crack at the assistant."

"Maybe you'd get further with women if you didn't use language like 'having a crack' at them," Reuben answered looking down his nose at Darius.

"Don't start acting superior with me, vampire. I'll kick your arse."

"Hang on, let me look when the next full moon is so I can book you in to do that." Reuben picked up his phone. "Oh look, you can't kick my arse for another few weeks. In the meantime, I'll keep you in my basement like a pet and drain your blood every evening, keep you half alive. I quite like wolf blood."

"Stop antagonizing him." I berated Reuben. "Take no notice, Darius. You know as well as we do that vampires can't drink much wereblood. It makes us volatile."

There had been quite a few twelve-step programmes set up for vampires before the truce had been called in Withernsea between vampires and weres. Reuben had been one of those who had to attend.

"So, when's your date?" asked Rav. "Please don't bring her back to Hanif's."

"Tomorrow evening, and about that." I looked at the others. "Any suggestions of where I could take her?"

Suggestions were made and then the game began in earnest. All thoughts of women and interspecies fighting were forgotten while us four men enjoyed a few simple games of cards.

Chapter Six

Shelley

It was time for our monthly meeting of *Female Entrepreneurs do it with their colleagues* and we'd closed the agency for an hour while we headed down to Jax's cafe.

She already had pots of tea and coffee on the large central table along with a selection of buns and cakes. The aromas were magnificent.

As we took our seats she nodded towards a woman with ginger bobbed hair. She sat behind us, drinking what looked like a strawberry milkshake.

"I told her we were closing at two for business, but she's not getting the idea." Jax scowled. "I hate that 'customer is always right' mantra. Why can't we accept that some customers are a pain in the arse?"

"Hell, she's wearing Louboutins," Ebony spoke, making all our heads turn to check out the woman's feet.

"If you don't do what I've asked you'll be fired." The woman spat down the phone.

We passed looks between ourselves.

"You think my temper's bad, wait until you meet the big boss." She yelled. "Now do what I asked and don't disturb me again, I'm busy."

She ended the call, threw her phone in her quilted Chanel handbag and then slowly sucked milkshake up a straw.

She broke off when she caught us looking at her. "Sorry, I'm a devil at being naughty. I realise you're waiting for me to finish. Just carry on, I won't listen. I'm almost done." She smiled, revealing a perfect white Hollywood style smile.

"It's fine. You enjoy your drink," said Jax, turning back to us and rolling her eyes. "Ow." Jax gripped her forehead, yelling in pain.

"What's the matter?" I asked placing a hand on Jax's shoulder.

"Stabbing pain in my eyes. I bet I'm coming down with a tension headache. It's the stress of running this business."

"Here," Ebony said, going in her handbag and taking out a small bottle of vodka. "This helps."

"Will you stop encouraging everyone to drink in the middle of the afternoon," I told her. "Seriously, Ebony. Do you need AA?"

"I don't drive," she said looking down at me.

"You know full well I'm referring to Alcoholics Anonymous, though I do worry you're having a breakdown."

"I don't get the voices when I drink vodka. I told you. It blocks them."

I looked across at Kim with a raised eyebrow. She twirled her finger at the side of her forehead.

"Well, enjoy your afternoon, ladies. I must be going," the customer said, scraping back her chair and rising from her seat. "It's a shame I'm not able to open a cafe at my place of work. It's too hot with the furnaces. Could have asked you to open a franchise of Jax's there. Oh well, maybe in the future I can corrupt you into it." She laughed. "In the meantime, I'll have to call in here more often. It's good to check out the local businesses, see if I have any competition." She looked at me as she said that. She couldn't own a dating agency, could she? Not if she had furnaces. She must own a smelting company or something.

"Well, ciao," she said and walked out of the door.

"Fricking bitch. No doubt from the new development near the Aldi," said Kim. "Scoping out the competition."

"I hope she's not thinking of opening a rival dating agency," I said.

"You're quiet, Ebony." I asked her.

"I'm getting one of my migraines. Something's trying to come through but my vodka consumption won't let it. We best hurry with this meeting before I have to go to lie down."

"Right, well first order of business," said Jax. "Are we all still okay with the open day in the cafe on Halloween? I'm going to do the obligatory buns with cobwebs and spiders and serve pumpkin lattes."

I made a gagging noise.

"Customers like them." Jax pouted.

"That's fine with us," Kim said. "I've ordered some new business cards to bring with us. Are we getting dressed up for the event?"

I groaned.

"Yes, we *all* have to get into the spirit of the event. Spirit, get it?" Jax clapped her hands at her own joke. "I'm dressing as a Zombie from *The Walking Dead*. What about you, Kim?"

"I think I'd look hot as a ghost. I have an idea for it already. Shelley can be a vampire in practice for when she becomes a real one. What about you, Ebony?"

"I'll come as an undead fortune teller."

"What about Samara? Could she not get away from the grooming salon?"

"She took the week off. Said last week was really busy after the full moon," Jax replied. "She's going to come as a pumpkin though. I've told her if she knocks my cups and plates off she's paying for any breakages."

"Oh, and are we going to the fireworks this year on

the beach? Apparently there's going to be a really good display and a bonfire," Kim said.

"I suppose so," I looked at the others and they shook their heads in agreement. There weren't many events in Withernsea so we felt we should make the most of the ones that came along.

"Anyway, what's this about you becoming a vampire?" said Jax.

"She's got a date with one. Tonight." Kim winked.

"I don't understand," said Jax.

"Theodore Landry. Total sex god but he thinks he's a vamp. The computer picked our Shelley as his ideal match. So she's off out on a hot date.

"Burning. Fire," drawled Ebony who was staring into space.

"I really need to get Frankie over here to take a look at her off the record," said Kim. nodding in Ebony's direction.

"Do you know, that's a good idea. Get him to drop by tomorrow morning if he can. I'm getting worried about her."

Ebony's eyes rolled, and the whites flashed. "You're one is here, but the path to true love is paved with danger."

"She really ought to sit with a crystal ball in the cafe, instead of behind that boutique counter." Jax shook her arm. "Ebony. EBONY, you drunk ass biatch. Get this coffee down you."

Ebony came to and swigged down the coffee, quickly following it with another one. "Thank you." Her shoulders loosened, then she pointed at Kim "You have a date with a police officer."

Kim pouted. "I do not. It wasn't me who had sex in the graveyard. There was no proof."

"Other than you left your panties there, which had your name sewn in them." I laughed.

"I can't help it if I like to go down the gym knowing which clothing is definitely mine. Someone must have nicked my clothes off the washing line."

Jax looked out of the window making me realise that there was some kind of disturbance outside. It sounded like arguing. "What's going on out there?" Jax said.

"I'll find out," said Kim. "Hold up." She pushed the door open and went outside.

"Should we let her go out on her own?" I bit my lip wondering whether I should see if Kim was okay when the lady herself stuck her body back halfway through the cafe door.

"Wow. Ebony, you better open your shop" She looked at me. "It looks like me and you better go help. That makeup set we showed Theo? There are about forty people outside wanting one. I told them you'd not hold that many in stock and they're willing to order, *and* I told them it was sixty quid, not thirty. Your day's looking up, Ebony."

Ebony brightened. "I knew that would be a winner."

"Saw it in the tea leaves did you?" I joked.

"No, last month's *InStyle*." She gave me a weird look.

"Well, we'd better go assist," I told Jax. "Thank you for the hospitality and for bringing us together as a business community."

"It's my pleasure," she said. "Now, enjoy your date tonight and just in case, wear a big scarf around your neck so he can't bite you."

"Yeah, okay."

"Where's he taking you, anyway?" she asked.

"No idea, but he seems a gentleman so I'm sure it'll be somewhere nice."

I should have kept my mouth shut.

Chapter Seven

Shelley

"A walk around a cemetery. Very original idea for a date," I told Theo as he guided me around.

"I read in a dating guide that you should take your girlfriend to meet your family. It shows your intentions are serious."

"That means living family, Theo. Ones you can be introduced to, you know? Get to know. They show you embarrassing pictures of you as a kid in your underwear."

"There are no such pictures of me. I could have some taken if that is acceptable?"

Fucking hell, yeah.

"So, Theo. Why don't you tell me a little about yourself? That's kind of a date thing, getting to know each other."

"But is it?" He pulled a face. "In these times of

social media I can consult Facebook and know what your life has been like for the last six years, and without being too insulting, might I say, your life has been extremely dull. Just constant selfies where you puff your lips out. I don't understand women at all, especially modern ones."

"Why do you want a wife anyway?"

"I want a family. My time is coming around again. I think 126 years is old enough to not have experienced fatherhood."

I took a step back, taking care not to fall in a newly dug grave. "You want a family? Not being funny but are you sure you're mentally stable enough for that?"

"My kind can procreate every one hundred and one years. I was turned at twenty-six, so my time will be in the New Year. Then it will be over for another one hundred and one years."

I rubbed at my forehead. I didn't even know where to start with this guy.

"Theo. Have you seen a doctor?"

"Yes, I'm in perfect health. My fake documents say I'm thirty and of course I can use the power of suggestion on my General Practitioner if he gets suspicious."

"The power of suggestion?"

"I guess you'd call it a kind of hypnotism. Basically, if humans get suspicious of my true nature, I can look into their eyes and make alternative suggestions."

"Really?" I scoffed.

"Yes, really. Shall I do it on you?"

"Okay. Make me believe that tree is a Celine handbag."

Theo stood still, got hold of my face and looked down into my eyes. He started chanting and then turned to the tree.

"Tell me what you see."

"The most beautiful handbag."

"See?"

"No, I don't. I'm lying. I see a fucking tree. Theo, I don't know why I like you but I do; however, you're full of shit."

"That's totally incorrect. Vampires are not made of fecal matter, and I need to try again because you should definitely think that tree is a bag."

He held my face again and looked deeply into my eyes. I had to admit that it gave me goose bumps. He was so gorgeous. Once again, he chanted.

"Okay, look at the tree."

My face twitched. "It's still a tree, Theo."

"Well, that explains it then." He clapped his hands and did a little skip which looked ridiculous on a six-foot-two man. "The only person a vampire is unable to coerce, according to our archives, is their one true love. You, my dearest Shelley, must be my one true love."

He got down on bended knee.

"Please would you do the honour of becoming my wife?"

"Easy, tiger," I told him, though I had to admit my goose bumps had goose bumps and I was feeling a little giddy. "Still on the first date here, getting to know each other, remember?"

"Ah, yes, my apologies. We have to do this the human way. How long does that normally take by the way, approximately?"

"Well, people can take as long as they like. I think the average is probably like two years."

"Two years? I can't wait that long. I'll miss my fertile window. My body clock is ticking."

"Well, it certainly needs to be longer than one date." I smiled. "Come on, I'm getting cold out here. Let's go for a burger. I'll meet your family another time."

We went to a local burger bar and I told him this was my treat. He gave me some cock and bull story about how he could enjoy food but it had no nutritional value—again. As I sat across from him I had to admit that something about him amused me. He wasn't boring that was for sure.

"So, tell me about your family, Shelley."

"There's not a lot to tell you about my real family. I was placed up for adoption when I was a baby. I was finally adopted when I was two years old. I don't remember anything about my parents. My adoptive parents got pregnant with a natural baby a month or so after they adopted me and they made my life a misery."

"Because you weren't their natural born?"

"They said I was cruel to my younger sister. I was no doubt jealous. I was almost three years old by the time they had Polly. Adoption takes time. All of a sudden there was another child there. I wasn't good enough anymore. They pushed me aside."

"I should like to visit them and kick their arse."

I burst out laughing. "You sound so weird saying that. You look so gentlemanly. Do you always wear a suit and shirt? I especially like your tie."

He looked down at his purple and black striped tie. My mind imagined it bound around my wrists. *OMG, stop it!*

"I enjoy being smart. But I can wear other clothing if that should please you. I have some jeans the shop assistant said hugged my arse and made it look like a peach. Is it a recent thing that shop assistants feel your derriere in clothes? This one did. He said it was how he ensured the jeans were a good fit."

"Oh my God, no. He made a pass at you." I started laughing. "Oh, Theo. What are we going to do with you? Were you kept in solitary confinement from birth? You know so much about some things and are so innocent with others."

"I grew up on the farm."

"Ah, yes. The farm. So, what's this about you trying to get it back?"

"My sire would have inherited the farm once my family was killed. But then he was killed by the farmhand so it went to his sire. I never met him but apparently, he sold it on Rightmove. I want it back, but the head of the household won't give it to me. He says if I want it I'll have to pay for it. He keeps ringing the police and having me removed from the property."

"What does he mean, pay for it? Is he blackmailing you?"

"No, it's back on Rightmove. He says he's had enough of me. It's been up for sale for a couple of years now. Every time someone goes to visit I do my suggestion thing on them on the way out so they think it's a wreck and the owner a pervert. I've hacked into the estate agency website so I know when the visits are."

"So why not just buy it?"

"It's a matter of principle. It was stolen from me. I shouldn't have to buy it."

"But the man who owns it wasn't your, erm, sire's sire."

"No, but he gave money to the sire. Money that should have been mine. I didn't ask to be bitten by a vampire and turned."

Theo went into a sulk and turned his head to look out of the window.

"Okay, then," I said. "Erm, fancy another coke?"

"I think I'd like to go home now."

I sat back in my chair surprised. "Theo, have I said something wrong?"

"It's talking about the farm. I get emotional about it."

"Look." I placed my hand on his. "I'm sure there's a way of getting it back. I'll help you, okay? We'll have to find this sire's sire."

"You'd do that? You'd help me get my farm back?"

"Weellll, I'll help you look into it further. See if there's a way of you owning it again. Do you have savings? Just in case we have to do a deal."

"I will not pay a penny for that property. Although yes, I have several million at my disposal."

Coke shot out of my nostrils.

"Pardon?"

Theo sighed. "Shelley, I've been around a long time. I've been a film star, a model. I've made a lot of money in that time. It's invested though, so don't think you can visit my place and find thirty grand under the sofa."

"I think we will call it a night. You've gone really moody. I've just got rid of my own PMT without encountering a male version."

"Males don't get PMT. We have no womb."

"It's called Petty Male Tantrum, and you own it tonight, pal." I felt my body tensing up.

"I do not." He looked out of the window again. Oh my God, what a prick.

"Yes, you do."

As my frustration mounted, Theo's glass slid across the table, gaining momentum before it upended straight down his shirt and the front of his trousers.

"Jesus, that's cold."

He grabbed a handful of napkins from the table and began dabbing at himself. "Well, would you look here. I said no food to be thrown at me, so you got me on a technicality, throwing a drink at me instead."

"I didn't do it." I protested, looking at the table legs to see if there was a wonky one.

"I suppose it just shot across the table and tipped over me," Theo said with dramatic hand gestures.

"Yes. Yes, it did. It was weird."

This date was going to hell in a handbasket. If I didn't rescue the situation I was going to put poor Theo off females for life.

"Stand up," I told him. I grabbed a few more napkins from the condiment table and started to dry his shirt, feeling his rock hard abs beneath the napkin.

Oh my.

"Erm. I think I'm dry now," he said just as a man in a suit approached us. The badge on his lapel identified him as the manager.

"I'm going to have to ask you to leave before I call the police. This is a family-friendly establishment, although thankfully there are currently no children present." The man's face was puce and his chin taut.

"What bug crawled up your arse? I'm only drying this man's-"

And then I realised, and I almost died. Without fully concentrating I'd moved downwards. My hand rubbing napkins over Theo's wet lap, and over his now rather erect cock.

"Oh my God." I reared back, at which point the help yourself drinks machines spurted juice everywhere. Fountains of black, orange and clear liquids rained over the restaurant floor.

"Oh my God. What is happening? What have you done, William?" The manager scurried off, shouting at the poor lad at the front who was innocently wrapping up a value meal.

"Something strange is going on," said Theo. "Only I find myself unable to concentrate as you are still rubbing my penis."

What the fuck was wrong with me? I'd started again. But it felt glorious beneath the napkins and it had been so long since I'd felt a man. I wanted him.

I took Theo's hand and dragged him outside of the restaurant.

"Can you try that suggestion thing on me again?"

"Yes, I'll suggest you never throw food or drink at me again." He leaned over me. The minute he was near enough I reached up and pressed my mouth to his. My warm lips met his cool ones. He really was going to have to see a doctor about his extremities. Maybe he had poor circulation?

Theo wrapped his arms around me and pulled me against him, against those hard abs I'd felt through the paper napkins. Now I was feeling them through my chest. There were too many clothes involved here.

And then a felt a little nip at my lip and a small wetness that Theo licked away. As he licked a heat seared up my groin. *Whoa. Calm down there. Pussy gone wild.* I placed my finger to my lip and looked at it. A small tinge of blood smeared my fingertip. "You bit me," I said, staring up at him and seeing his descended fangs.

"How do you make those come down?" I said, reaching up and touching them. Then I pulled at them, and realised that they weren't fake at all.

"You really are, you really are..." My breath came faster than I could process it and I went increasingly dizzy.

"Told you it always takes a third time," he said as he swept me up and away. That was the last I knew as everything went black.

CHAPTER Eight

Shelley

When I came around I was in my house laid on the sofa, with Theo sat at the other end looking at me with concern.

"Oh, thank goodness. Any longer and I would have called for a doctor," he said, stroking my forehead.

"How long was I out?"

He lifted his arm to look at his watch. "Oh, around a minute and a half."

I stuck my head forward. "Theo, my house is thirteen minutes away from the burger place—by car."

"We didn't travel by car," Theo answered. "Now, how are you feeling?"

I scrunched up my forehead. Why was I back here, anyway? What had happened? Oh yeah, I'd been kissing Theo and... and... he'd grown fucking fangs.

I scooted to the edge of the sofa, tucking my arms around my knees.

"You're a vampire!"

"Yes. I think I told you that in my application, and again at dinner–where I thought you'd begun to believe me-then again at the second interview and once more earlier, where you felt my fangs and fainted."

"But it's not possible."

"Why isn't it?"

"Because you're made up. You don't exist."

"It's very conceited to believe that you, as a human female, can exist, but I, as a vampire male, must be some kind of an illusion. I've just as much right to be around here as you have. Anyway, you weren't complaining when I was kissing you."

"When you bit me slightly."

"I got excited. I don't have to do that but it is quite enjoyable, for both of us."

I remembered the feeling I'd had-fire down below.

"And what about sex? Do you do anything different from a human male?"

"No, other than to say I lost my virginity at sixteen years old, which means I have one hundred and ten years of sexual experience. I've picked up a trick or two in that time." He winked.

My stomach fluttered.

My heart beat faster.

My vajayjay went *cooommmeeee oonnnnn*.

And I launched myself at him.

He pushed me away and held me at arm's length with what I felt to be considerable strength from arm-porn arms that made Captain America's look like shoelaces. "Are you sure you're feeling up to this?"

"Hell yeah," I announced, and that was it. He brought me back to him and crushed his lips to mine.

His mouth trailed down my neck, eliciting goose bumps as his cool touch felt like the tickle of a feather upon my skin. Theo stripped off his jacket, and I undid his tie, throwing it aside and then unbuttoning his shirt. There were so many buttons, by the time I got to about four away from the bottom, Theo helped me by ripping it straight off, buttons pinging everywhere.

I raised my arms as he lifted my top over my head, leaving me in a white lacy bra.

The sound of my heavy breathing filled the room. I realised Theo's didn't. I wrapped my hands around the back of his neck and pulled him closer, kissing him again and then I rested my head in the crook of his neck, waiting for the tell-tale rise and fall of his chest. It didn't come.

He wasn't breathing.

Ah well. Some of my dates acted more brain dead than Theo. I'd worry about it after I'd had my wicked way with him.

I unfastened the button at the top of his jeans and he lifted his hips up as I pulled them off his legs. Then I took his socks off. That left just his boxer briefs, and I prayed to God that the bulge in his pants wasn't a hot dog he'd stolen from the burger bar and saved for later.

Placing my fingers at the edge of his pants I pulled them down.

His dick sprang up—what must have been a good ten inches of it. It almost took out my eye.

Holy mother of God, not all of him was dead.

I was still in my skirt and I quickly slipped it off, leaving me in my bra and lacy thong. Then I pushed Theo back against the sofa and took him in my mouth, and yes, I had to open wide.

He groaned.

"Your mouth. It's so warm against my skin. Vampire women's mouths are cold."

I let him slip back out. "If you mention other women again while I'm doing this, you'll find you're not the only one who can bite," I told him.

"Fair point," he said. "As I was saying, your mouth is so warm. It feels amazing. Best ever."

Now he was talking. I was the best ever giver of head. You betcha, mate. I swirled my tongue around that baby and sucked on him like I was in a top porn movie until I heard his groans increase.

He moved away from me, then lifted me and carried me upstairs. He pushed open my bedroom door after I pointed to it, taking me inside where he placed me on the bed. There, he removed my bra and thong and positioned himself over me, moving down and catching a breast in his mouth. He bit on my nipple and that same sensation flooded through me. There must be something in his saliva. Holy guacamole, what was it going to do to me when he went down there?

I was about to find out. He lowered himself so he was between my thighs and then his cool tongue licked up my seam. It was like he'd been sucking on an ice cube. The sensations were exquisite. He nipped on my bud and my thighs came off the bed with such force that if he hadn't reared back, I might have knocked him unconscious. Then I wondered, could you make an undead person unconscious? *I don't care* screamed my clitoris as Theo went back to town on me, licking and sucking until I felt the pressure build and exploded into his mouth.

Dear Lord. I apologise for all the cursing and blaspheming but I've never experienced anything like it.

Then he was back above me and lining himself up at my core. He pushed inside. I was about to remind him about a condom but then I remembered he wasn't fertile until January.

"Hey," I interrupted, and he stopped, staring into my eyes. "God, he was fucking gorgeous."

"Thanks," he said, and I realised I'd said it out loud. Crap! "Can I carry on now?"

I shook my head. "That wasn't it. Do you have

health checks? Are you free from diseases, you know, like the clap?"

"I don't have any diseases, Shelley. I'm technically dead and disease free." His mouth turned up at the corners in a smirk. "Anything else?"

"Nope." I shook my head. "We're good to goooooooo."

He'd pushed inside me before I'd finished my sentence and filled me to the brim with that magnificent cock of his. I seriously wanted to ask him to pause and withdraw so I could get up and do a little dance of smugness. His head moved to the side of my neck as he thrust inside me and once again goose bumps rose across my skin. The sensations across my skin and between my legs were so good it was beyond explanation. He worked us into a frenzy, my hips meeting every thrust until I felt him stiffen and my own climax build. And then he bit my neck.

He bit my neck as he came inside me and it was like stars floated and unicorns danced. Rainbows must have surrounded me and angels must have sung as I came, and came, and came. Yes, three times with aftershocks like no earthquake could ever hope to produce.

I think he killed me.

And I was happy to have died.

He gathered me into his arms and snuggled under the covers with me. I felt sleep overtake me. He kissed my forehead and whispered, "I'll stay until you're sound asleep and then I'll have to leave. I need to go back to where I'm safe while I slumber."

"Okay," I said, and I drifted off thinking that if he'd proposed again right now, the slapper in me would have said yes.

∼

"Shelley!"

Oh God, not this again. I opened my eyes and looked around. Theo wasn't there in bed with me anymore. I was totally alone. Well, apart from the weird woman sitting on a black chaise longue this time. Where did I make this dream shit up?

"You're not dreaming, Shelley. We need you to realise that you're in danger. Also, you're getting your powers back and you need to be aware of this."

I sat up and stared the woman down. "What are you talking about?"

"Shelley. I'm your mother. Now whether you believe me or not right now—and if you could, that would really help—I need you to listen. I'm a witch. You are part-witch. Your father was a human man, and he made a deal with her to secure your safety."

"A deal with who?"

"Lucy. She agreed not to look for you if your father went with her. It was a trick. She just wanted him. Wanted to split us up. I warned the Linley's that you might exhibit

some signs of magic, and if you did they needed to get a witch or wizard to put a binding spell on you. I gave them the number of a friend. They must have done this as I've not detected you until this past week. But this week you've done something. Something that's disturbed her. The warnings are that she's about to leave her chambers and come looking for the cause of the disturbance."

I slapped myself in the face a few times. It was bad enough I had slept with a vampire and had the whole undead thing to deal with. I couldn't process this dream shit too. Fantasy needed to stay away right now, real life was enough.

"Shelley."

Oh God she was still there.

"Shelley, I'm not a dream. I'm IN your dream. I've told you this already. Look, go see the Linley's. Let them tell you the truth and then we can talk again. But please be careful. She doesn't want people to be happy. Withernsea has been her pet for years. She didn't care while you were matchmaking humans, said it gave her the chance of extra recruits, but she wants you to leave the supernaturals alone. They're her toys. And she doesn't know who you are yet. That you're our daughter."

"Who is this goddamn Lucy bitch?" I shouted. "She sounds like she has a right attitude."

My dream mother looked at me with a great deal of anxiety on her face.

"I told you. Lucy. Lucy Fir. The head of Hell."

I woke up.

What the fuck was that dream? I hoped all sex sessions with Theo wouldn't give me nightmares, although truth be told he hadn't boffed me when I'd had the first one. Recurrent dreams, hey? I must have things on my mind. Well, the first thing on my mind was to make myself a massive cup of coffee because last night's shenanigans had worked up quite a thirst.

I headed down to the kitchen, feeling a satisfying ache within my thighs. I'd had sex! Extremely amazing sex! Whoo hoo! I made a fresh pot of coffee and then wandered into the lounge with a mug before jumping and tipping half the thing down my front. For fuck's sake, this was becoming quite the habit.

I stared at what had made me jump. In the middle of my room was a flame. Just hanging there in midair. As I moved closer to it, the flame turned into smoke, black wisps forming the words:

You were warned.

The words dissipated and then it was like none of it had ever been there. Was I sleep deprived and had imagined it? Maybe having sex with a vampire had drained some of my life energy or something. I couldn't even talk about it with anyone, could I? Who'd believe me?

I went upstairs to change. At least I didn't have to spend money on a new top at Ebony's this time.

Oh. That was it. I needed to talk to Ebony. Maybe crazy Ebony was not so crazy after all.

Chapter Nine

Ebony

I'd wondered when Shelley was going to realise I wasn't the alcoholic nutcase she thought I was. Being a seer was draining, especially if warnings and messages about someone very close to you were coming. Vodka wasn't my drug of choice, it was a necessity to get through the day if I didn't want to be pestered by the voices.

I'd started having impressions about Shelley a couple of weeks ago. First it was just the odd sweeping of words into my mind.

Her one is coming.

She's awakening.

This was followed by feelings of edginess when she was close. Like the balance of something was out of kilter.

But as she walked into my boutique this morning,

the blast into my mind almost knocked me to the ground. I held my head until the pain ebbed away.

"Ebony. Are you okay?"

"Give me a moment," I said, taking a seat behind my counter. "It's the thoughts and visions. They come too fast sometimes."

"Do you need your vodka?" Shelley asked, and I stared at her.

Do you need your vodka? Not berating me for drinking. Something had changed.

It was time for me to do my thing.

"Could you pass me your hand?" I told her, "and no matter what you see happen to me, do not let go of it. Understand me? If you want answers, that's how we get them."

"Okay," she said, biting on her lip before holding out her hand.

I took it and centred myself, asking for protection before I opened myself up. The messages and visions kicked in and I knew that to Shelley my face would have taken on a grey pallor.

Finished. I closed myself down and thanked the angels for their protection. Then I opened my eyes.

"Jeez. I'm glad your colour is returning. I thought you were dying on me," said Shelley, concern etched in her features.

"I have to straddle the line between life and death. It's draining," I told her. "Now. You and Theo. He is your one. You can take your time. You can deny it, but they scream it at me."

"Who's they?" Shelley leaned forward sliding her chair even closer.

"I don't know. Beings so high they don't have a face, just a presence. They tell me you are in danger though. That you are at risk of death."

"Well, duh? Theo will want to make me a vampire won't he, if I stay with him?"

I shook my head. "No, that is not who intends to harm you. Your agency is causing a change in Withernsea. There are those who oppose it."

"I've been having weird dreams, Ebony. This woman says she's my real mum and that I'm half a witch and that the head of Hell is after me. That's not real, right? That's me having a bad dream."

My eyes widened in shock. "You upset the devil?"

"I guess so, but only in my dreams, yeah. Apparently, she's called Lucy, and she's pissed with me."

I tried to gain traction on my thoughts but couldn't hold onto anything. "I don't know if it's her. I feel like there's more to this. Another presence. Tell me more about these dreams."

Shelley explained about seeing her mum twice and that she'd been told to visit her adoptive parents. That her powers were emerging now she'd embraced the supernatural world.

"And then there was the flame this morning."

"Flame?"

"Yeah, one flame hanging in the middle of the room, then it puffed out, and a message said 'you were warned'."

I gripped the edge of the table. "That is one of hell's calling cards."

"What am I going to do?" she panicked. "I upset the devil. Who does that? I'll be burned alive!" Shelley started pacing around the shop picking up different clothes. "I might as well max my credit cards if I'm not going to survive the night."

"Look, let's say these dreams are real and not dreams. Your mum said you should visit your adoptive parents. That's a start. Go see what they have to say to you. Why not tell Theo? Maybe you could take him along with you for support? If you're getting threats, you need the police."

"Oh yeah, 'dear policeman, I've seen a flame hanging in midair. Can you check it out?' I'll be carted off to an asylum."

"There's a secret branch of the force," I told her. "I'll make some calls. Now, if it's true you're part-witch, you'll need to ask someone, a witch or wizard for guidance. Maybe your mum could help? You need to learn some simple protection spells. I have ones for opening and closing myself to spirits but they aren't going to help you."

"Thank you, Ebony." Shelley touched my arm. "I'm

sorry for thinking you were insane and an alcoholic. You've been so very kind. Now, I've just found out I might be half-witch, I'm shagging a vampire, and the devil is after me, so could I please have a vodka?"

"You shagged Theo?"

"I did." A massive smile broke out on Shelley's face. "And it was heavenly." She sighed. "Bloody hell, Ebony. What am I going to do?"

Bloody hell indeed.

Chapter Ten

Shelley

It was 10am before I made it into the office. Yes, we worked Saturdays but only until lunchtime. Arriving late was so unlike me but hey ho. The sound of muffled laughter came from Kim's office and I walked towards it and knocked on her door.

"Come in," she shouted.

I walked in to see her lipstick smudged across her face and her cheeks pink. In front of her was a good looking blonde-haired guy. I presumed this was the good doctor.

"I'm Shelley, the owner of Withernsea Dating, and you are?"

"Dr Francis Love. My friends call me Frankie." His green eyes flashed with a touch of mischief. "I'm sorry to come here causing mayhem. Your assistant left something at mine. I wanted to return them to her." He went into his pocket and pulled out a pair of panties.

"How did they get there?" Kim looked astounded and looked down the top of her trousers. "I could swear I put those on this morning."

He threw them at her and gave me a wink. I rolled my eyes. The man was a moron.

"Well. Nice to meet you, Dr Love," I said, making sure he knew exactly how friendly I felt towards him. "Kim. Could you go get us some coffee and a couple of doughnuts from Jax's? I'll see you in my office in fifteen?"

"Yes, Boss." She was still looking down her trousers.

"And you might want to put some pants on," I told her before stomping out of the room.

A knock came at my door not a minute later. "Come in." I sighed. I really needed that coffee.

Frankie strolled in, the door closing behind him as he walked in front of me. "Oh Shelley, it seems we got off on rather the wrong foot."

I rubbed my forehead. I did not need this tosser this morning when I was trying to work out how to get the devil off my back.

"We're fine. You can go now." I pointed at the door.

He pointed at my head and a wispy tendril of what looked like white smoke unfurled into the air from my temple, not dissimilar to what had happened with the flame earlier. The words revealed themselves one by one before disappearing into thin air.

Tosspot.

Knobhead.

Get out fucktard.

~

"Oh dear. I really haven't made a good first impression, have I?" A comfy cushion appeared on the seat in front of me, along with a matching footstool and he sat down. "I can smell you, you know. It's delicious."

"Fuck off, pervert," I shouted, and the footstool whipped across the room, smashing into the door.

"Ooh, yes, we need to get a handle on that. I can smell your magic, darling. Not your pussy. No, you've sullied that thing by poking the vampire."

"How do you know I've been with a vampire?"

"I'm not giving away all my secrets. We've only just met. Tell me, have you had any more episodes of things flying around with your temper? You could hurt someone if you don't get it under control."

I cleared my throat. "Are you saying I did that?" I pointed to the footstool.

"Yes, and untrained magic is dangerous. But not to worry because I can help you."

"Oh my God. You're a supe too? Is there anyone here who isn't?" I pursed my lips together.

"Kim isn't. The coffee shop woman, Jax, she's not. Ebony's a seer. You're a witch. I'm a wizard. It was so funny seeing Kim's face when I magicked her panties off her body into my hand."

My mouth dropped open, and I rubbed my eyebrow. "I'm really part supe?"

"Yes. It's very faint, but there's definitely a smell of magic emanating from your pores. Now, it's in my best interests to teach you how to handle it. Otherwise you're going to out us all and some of us like to fly under the radar—and no, you don't get a broomstick. That's just stereotyping."

"Did you read my thoughts then? Because that's not okay?" I pouted.

He sighed, looking weary. "I'm a wizard not a psychic. I said the word fly. The natural association of that word to a new witch is broomstick. It's so predictable."

I folded my arms across myself. "You're annoying."

"I am, and yet I'm going to help you. Be at mine at 6pm this evening for your first lesson."

"I'm making plans for this evening. I have a date and might be seeing family."

"Not tonight you're not. Do you want to cause people harm?"

I shook my head.

"I thought not." He walked over to my desk and flicked his fingers near my notepad. His address appeared on it.

"Hey, can you teach me a protection spell?" I asked him.

"Hmm, you pissed someone off already? Can't imagine that with your uber friendly demeanour."

"Bite me," I spat.

"Getting me confused with the boyfriend again. Yes, I can teach you a simple protection spell."

"Will it protect me from evil?"

He tilted his head at me. "How evil?"

I held my hand out in front of me. "If this is evil, then" – I raised my arm as high as it would go – "then way, way, way, up here evil."

"Demonic?"

"Like the head of Hell."

He exhaled loudly and grabbed my hand. "Then you mean way, way, way down here." He pulled my hand to the floor, almost toppling me over.

"Mine at 6pm. You can't afford not to make it."

The door opened and as Kim walk inside he vanished into thin air.

Holy fuck.

"Sorry about that," Kim said. "Frankie turned up first thing. We did have a snog but I wouldn't shag in the office. I could swear I put my knickers on this morning. We're really going to have to try sleeping when I see him. Its messing with my head."

"Don't worry about it. I'm not sleeping well either," I said and then I winked.

Kim placed the coffees and doughnuts on the table. "You dirty mare. Tell me all about it," she said. So, I did.

The problem with a vampire lover was that I couldn't phone him in the morning. I had to wait until after 4pm. I called his mobile and a lazy, sexy arsed drawl came from the other side. "Shelley." I swear to God if my name had been a chocolate fondant that gooey centre had just dripped out and my tongue was licking that bitch.

"Hey, Theo. Good sleep?"

"Hmm, wicked dreams," he said and my core pulsed. "So, what are you doing tonight? I think I need more dating help."

"Nice try," I told him. "That's why I'm calling. I can't do tonight. Some things have happened." I filled him in on recent events.

"Ah, that explains how I ended up doused in coke."

"Yeah, I'm sorry about that. Looks like I have anger management issues that need addressing."

"Are you really sorry, Shelley? It led to the most

pleasant evening I've spent in a long time. And when I say a long time..."

"Yeah, maybe tens of years. I get it. You're really old. Good point though. No, I'm not the slightest bit sorry. It does mean that I need to have a little lesson in managing my temper."

"Oh, now magic. It smells like turnips or sprouts to me. Thinking back, there was an odour, I thought you or one of the other patrons had flatulence," he said. "So, who is giving you this lesson about magic?"

"Kim's boyfriend, Frankie."

"Oh, Dr Love."

"You know Frankie?"

"Yes, his odour is most unsavory. I'd suggest a name change to Frank Lee Hestinks, if I was his mother.

"Theo. Are you being bitchy?"

"It's the stench. It's unbecoming."

"Well I hope I don't start to smell like that. It'll put a blot on our date nights."

"We're having date nights?" he said.

"Oh, I should think so."

He laughed. "You're falling in love with me."

"Steady on, we've only had one date."

"Yes, but admit it. You love my mouth, my fingers and my cock so we're getting there body part by body part."

"Theodore Landry! I thought you were a gentleman. Where's this naughty boy come from?"

A deep hearty chuckle came down the line.

"So, I'll definitely escort you to your parents' house tomorrow. Would you do me a favour and make an appointment to view the farm next week? I'd like to show you where we're going to raise our children."

"Theo!"

"Yes, I know. I'm doing it again. That's how I scare women away. But I can't help myself with you, Shelley. There's something about you, like we're meant to be."

"Well I'm meant to be at Frankie's at six and I want to grab a bite to eat first so I'd better get a move on."

"You might want to have to have a bath in some extra strong scented bath soak before I see you tomorrow," Theo said. "If all else fails, expect to be Febreezed as soon as I see you."

"You're just so romantic, Theo. See you tomorrow."

I rang the bell of Frankie's self-detached bungalow. I'd thought being a wizard he'd have a dark mansion with turrets and cobwebs everywhere.

He answered the door, took one look at my face and huffed. "I have bad knees, can't do with stairs and my housekeeper has obsessive-compulsive disorder."

"Me thinks I need to learn how to have a game face before spells," I told him before following him into his lounge.

A black cat walked up to me and weaved around my legs. "Aww, you're so pretty."

"Scoot, Maisie," he said, and the cat showed Frank her ass, gave a hiss and scurried out of the room.

I raised an eyebrow. "Wizard with a black cat?"

"Coincidence," he told me. "Just happened to pick that colour. So, I made a fresh pot of coffee and I bought some of your favourite chocolate doughnuts. Let me just bring them through."

He was starting to grow on me. Well his bribes were. I helped myself to a doughnut.

"So, how much of your magic are you aware of?"

"That'll be, well, how to put it, shit bugger all," I told him. "I may have upended a drink on someone, may have caused drinks to spurt out of a machine, may have thrown a footstool. Or..." I paused. "The table wobbled, and the drink fell over; the drinks machine had a fault; and you kicked the stool."

"Only one thing for it then. Let me get a ball."

He placed a ball on a small coffee table in front of me. "Keep your mind on this, not on the coffee or doughnuts. I have expensive carpets."

I focused my eyes on the ball. It was a small orange-coloured, light plastic and more than likely belonged to Maisie.

"Okay. Relax your mind and move the ball."

I stared at it and willed it to shift. Nothing.

"Keep trying."

Nothing.

"Hmmm. Maybe it only surfaces when you have heightened emotions. Like when I annoyed you earlier, and the footstool went out. That means your powers are quite weak. Pathetically weak."

The ball flew off the chair, sailed around Frankie's head and hit him on the nose. "Who are you calling weak, you sexist pig?"

Frankie chuckled. "Okay, I think we established it's tied to your emotions. Fact. So, I'm going to teach you a spell that will keep you protected from outside harm. Say it every morning and every evening."

"How will I remember it?"

"I'll write it down," he said. "But practice it until you know it by heart."

"Thank you. I'm sorry we got off on the wrong foot."

"Not to worry. I have a feeling we're going to be spending a lot more time together as your powers grow. Now, just one thing. I know you have no reason to believe me, but the vampire. Please tread carefully. Don't ever forget he's a killer."

I looked at him with narrowed eyes. "Thanks for the advice but I can handle my own love life, and while we're on the subject let's talk about yours. Let me tell you, if you hurt my friend you'll have me to contend with, and with that level of untrained anger who knows what I'd do to you."

Frankie flinched at my words. "I only thought it prudent to remind you. The vampire killed his own family, his own kin whom he must have loved dearly, so don't be so complacent as to think that a half-breed like you is safe."

I sighed. "Sorry. I do understand what you're saying, Frankie. I'll ensure to say my spells to keep myself from danger."

He nodded. "Some beings are too strong for the spells, Shelley. You'll need to harness your magic to free yourself of them. But more on that another time."

I finished my coffee and stood up. "Thank you for this," I said. "I do appreciate your offer of help."

He smiled. "It's no problem at all. Let Kim know that I missed seeing her tonight."

"I will."

"Did she say what she was doing? I had a bad feeling, like she might have another date." He looked at the floor.

"She didn't say so."

"Okay, well night then."

I walked out of his house and caught the bus back home. I couldn't work out what I thought about him, so instead, I got out the expensive bottle of Jo Malone bath soak I'd purchased before I went to Frankie's and soaked in the tub for two hours. There was no way I wanted Theo thinking I smelled like turnips.

I slept without dream interruptions from family members. I called in for coffee at Jax's before heading to the office. Kim had sent me a text saying she'd had an emergency and would be in as soon as she could.

About ten minutes after I got there, she arrived. I went through to her office with the still quite hot drink.

"Thought you might need this? Oh, what's happened to your neck?"

She touched the piece of gauze and tape on her neck. "I've been bitten by something and the damn thing won't stop itching. I got some insect bite cream from the pharmacy but it's not doing anything. It's driving me mad."

"Let me see," I instructed her.

She removed the gauze and I gaped. The puncture wounds on her neck looked exactly like a vampire bite. The skin around it was raised and red, and she was definitely having a reaction to it.

"Let me get the first aid kit and clean it up."

I went into my office for the kit. Shit, how had she got bitten? She clearly remembered none of it. I would have to ask Theo if there were any rogue vampires on the loose. But first, I'd have to question Kim to see if she'd had a secret date last night.

I wandered back into her office with some salt water in a bowl and some cotton wool. I dipped the cotton wool in the salty solution then squeezed it and applied it to her neck.

"Christ, it won't stop itching. I'm going to scratch my own neck off."

"Hold still."

For some reason, I felt the need to rub my fingers over the bites. I couldn't describe it. It was like an inner suggestion to do it and there was a strange tingle to my fingers. I placed one finger over each of the wounds and thought about healing them. When I took my fingers away, the bites were almost closed.

"What did you do? The itching has stopped. Oh, thank fuck." Kim moved her head from side to side and then stretched. "God that is so much better. I could kiss you."

"It was the salt water," I lied. "Then I held my fingers over the bites to create a seal. I'm going to put a plaster over it now and then we'll do the same again after lunch to make sure it stays okay."

"Oh my God, I can't thank you enough. It was enough to make me go drown myself."

Things were getting serious. The threats were one thing but some vampire had toyed with my friend. I needed answers, and I needed them quickly. "Did you go out last night? I thought you were having a lazy evening."

"That's exactly what I did. I didn't go anywhere. Sat watching TV until ten and then I had an early night."

She lifted a large bag from behind her. "I'm just going to pop out to the launderette. There's obviously something in my sheets that bit me. I'm never leaving it a month between washing my bedding again." She opened the bag and pulled out a tie. "Do you have to hand wash designer ties?"

My mouth gaped open for a second time.

"Where did you get that?"

"It was on the floor by my bed. Frankie must have dropped it during one of our sessions. I thought I'd get it laundered."

"Can I look at it?" I asked her.

"Sure." She passed it to me.

I held the purple and black striped tie in my hand and turned it over. It had splashes of a dark liquid on it and I held it to my nose. Coca-cola.

"I'll sort this out for you. You have to be really careful with designer stuff. Might take me a couple of days," I said. "You go now while it's quiet."

"Okay." She hopped off her chair. "See you in ten."

She left the office, and I sat back on her desk. Bite marks and Theo's tie? What was going on? Had my vampire boyfriend really attacked my friend?

CHAPTER Eleven

Shelley

Theo arrived to pick me up from my house at six. I'd done a protection spell on myself to ward off any evil spirits so if he reacted to me, I'd know he was a suspect.

I opened the door and leaned towards him to give him a kiss and he hissed and jumped away from me.

"God, I knew it. Why did you bite my friend? You utter bastard!" I was so enraged Theo whipped into the air as if taken by a sudden gust of wind. He hit his car with a loud thud.

"Ouch. Fuck that hurt." He stood up clutching his back. "It's a good job I'm already dead. What did you do that for?"

"You bit my friend," I yelled. "Were you trying to kill her? Turn her? Or were you just hungry?"

He tilted his head and stared at me with narrowed eyes. "I'm sorry about my reaction. You've done magic haven't you, because you smell like refuse, like soiled nappies to be precise. I'm not sure how to proceed with our outing. Do you have a peg for my nose? I don't need to breathe. I just need to stop the smell going up it. It's not really a look I want to continue going forwards though. I kind of like my dapper, designer clothed, and smooth self."

"Ah yes, talking about designer clothing, excuse me a moment." I disappeared into the house. When I came back out, I dangled his tie in front of him.

"I wondered where that went. You're distracting me with your beautiful face and body. At least I only left my tie behind, not my trousers, hey? That would have got me some strange looks."

"You left it at Kim's," I told him. "Along with another souvenir of your visit."

"Kim's? I don't even know where she lives."

"Well, she found your tie next to her bed, and she had two puncture wounds on the side of her neck that I had to heal this morning."

Theo crossed his arms across his body. "I can assure you that this was not my doing, if that's what you are trying to insinuate?"

"What other explanation is there? Bite marks and your tie in her room?"

"How about if I was set up?" He looked at me and disappointment crossed his features. "You are so quick to judge me guilty. I can see in your face that you don't believe me."

I glare at him. "You'll have to excuse me, Theo. It's the whole you're a vampire, I'm a witch, Frankie's a wizard shit that's going on. Ebony's a seer, my mother comes to me in dreams. I can't handle all this right now. I don't know what's going on and I feel like I'm going crazy." Feeling tears threaten, I looked down at the floor and then back up.

"Look, I'm going to visit my parents on my own, Theo. Thanks for the offer to come and to drive, but I'll get the train. I think it's better that I don't see you for a couple of days. Just until I get my head together."

Theo stared at me. Anger flared in his eyes, a quick flash of red appeared and then left. "I'm disappointed in today's events but as you wish. I'm not sure I could have shared a confined space with you, anyway. The fact remains that we have a problem because I'm not sure I can date someone who smells like they have terrible flatulence. Go to see your family. I hope they provide some of the answers you're looking for. You know where I am if you wish to speak to me again." He turned around and walked away.

There was a lump in my throat. I had been quick to judge him but what other explanation could there be? I pushed the thought to the back of my mind. Right now, I needed to focus on information gathering. Train timetables needed to be consulted as the Linley family were expecting me at eight.

Mark and Debbie Linley lived in a three-bedroomed semi in Hull. As I arrived at the entrance to the driveway, I spotted cobwebs surrounding the house. It was covered in them. What the fuck was going on? I stood at the front door and pulled strings of the web away, pressing on the doorbell.

My adopted dad answered the door. He shone with an orange glow. If they turned out to be supernatural too, I would admit myself to a psychiatric unit on my way home.

"Why is your house covered in cobwebs?" I asked, clearing some away to enter the house.

"You can see them?" he asked, his eyes wide.

"Well, duh, it'd be hard not to. Ever thought of getting the place cleaned up? You might need to employ someone if you have a spider infestation."

He sighed. "Come through, Shelley. We need to talk."

I followed him through to the living room. It had been decorated since I was last there and looked really nice. Brown leather sofas, a cream carpet and some rose gold ornaments gave it a modern feel.

"The place is looking good, Mum," I told the woman sitting on the sofa. She'd had her hair cut since I'd seen her last, with it now in a short brown bob. She looked at me, a smile hovering on her lips, like she wanted to welcome me but couldn't bring herself to do so.

"She can see the webs," my dad told her.

"Fuck," said my mum.

"Er, language?" I hadn't been allowed to swear when I was home. In fact, I hadn't been allowed to do most things. Largely I'd been confined to my bedroom and lived my life out of their way.

"Anyway, you're being so welcoming, folks. It's a pleasure as always."

My dad rubbed his forehead. "Yes, well, sometimes you decide to adopt a kid, and you don't get what you were expecting."

My heart sank in my chest. They didn't even try to hide their disappointment.

"I'm sorry I'm not the daughter you wanted me to be. I'm not sure what I did wrong, but I guess that's why I'm here, so shall we head past the bullshit politeness and get down to what I need to know about my childhood. Do you know about my real parents? Only I'm having a few problems right now and need some answers."

My parents looked at each other. "Take a seat, Shelley," my mother said. "We have quite a bit to tell you."

I sat down on a chair opposite them. "You'll have to excuse us a minute," my mum said, and they closed their eyes before launching into an incantation. They spoke in unison and the glow around them grew brighter still. They stopped and looked at me.

"Who are you protecting yourself from?" I asked.

"You," they replied.

"Excuse me?" My eyes widened. "Why would you need to protect yourself from me?"

My mother sighed.

"When we decided we wanted to adopt, we found it was rather more difficult than we thought. The adoption agency told us it would take years to be accepted. We'd made our peace with this, and then our keyworker phoned to say she had a child for us. You." She pointed to me as if I didn't know who I was. "We came to visit you and you looked so adorable, with your red hair. We fell in love and after visiting with you a few times we agreed to adopt you."

"Okay, this all sounds perfectly normal."

"But before your adoption went through, we went to the agency and were escorted through to a room where we met your real mother. It was apparent, more or less straight away, why you were being adopted. They'd told us your father had left her, and she had mental health issues. She was babbling about a devil taking her husband and that we were to protect her child."

I swallowed. "What did she look like?"

"She had long dark black hair with a white streak through it. Of course, we thought she was deranged.

The meeting was brought to a halt because of her distress and we didn't see her again."

I closed my eyes for a moment. Was this because she'd been taken to another realm or had I just inherited a mental health problem? I wasn't sure which reality was worse.

My mother continued. "As your adoption progressed, you asked me why you had a new mummy. I told you that yours was poorly and that you'd been sent to be my special daughter as I couldn't have a baby of my own. That my tummy was broken." A tear came to my mum's eye. "You placed your hands on my stomach and closed your eyes and you said, 'please mend my new mummy's tummy'. A couple of months later my pregnancy with Polly was confirmed. We'd heard that this happened a lot, you adopted and got naturally pregnant. They put it down to us relaxing about conception."

"But?"

"You kept singing. About the baby sister who was coming. In time, we found out that we were expecting a girl. You told me she'd be born a month early, but I wasn't to worry, to just take you to the hospital and you'd make sure she was okay. That your magic was strong. I started to feel a little edgy as your mum had talked about you having magic. We'd put it down to her being crazy.

"Polly arrived prematurely, and she struggled to

breathe. Things were touch and go and I begged your father to bring you. You looked through the incubator, closed your eyes and said 'she's okay now', and she was." My mum was openly crying now. "I felt like I had been given two miracles. You, and Polly."

"So, what went wrong?"

My mother sobbed, incapable of talking, so my dad took over.

"Babies need a lot of attention, and I guess because Polly was our natural born, she got even more. We're not proud of that but, of course, we'd see the family resemblance in her, something that couldn't happen with you. We saw her first smile, her first teeth. You were young, and became very jealous." He took a deep breath. "We walked into Polly's bedroom one day and she was hovering above the cot. You'd opened a window, and said she needed to leave. That she was ruining everything. We got you to place her back into the cot and while your mum hugged you, I phoned the number your mother had handed me before she'd been taken away. A man answered the phone and said he'd been expecting my call. He came straight around and he placed a ward of protection around us. To those with magic, it looks like cobwebs. We can't see it."

"Oh," I said.

"The man waited until you slept and then he bound you with a spell that suppressed your magic. He reassured us that it likely wouldn't appear again although there were no guarantees."

"So we kept you away from us and Polly," my mum said between sobs. "We weren't proud of what we did but we needed to keep her safe. To keep ourselves safe."

"You ignored me!" A vase wobbled precariously on the sideboard while the webs flashed with silver sparks and glowed brighter. They looked at each other and anxiety etched across their faces.

And then I understood and everything calmed.

"I can't excuse what you did. You turned your love away from me and only gave it to Polly. You distanced yourself from me. But I understand now why you did it. You were afraid. I wouldn't have harmed Polly. I remember opening that window because she was hot. I don't remember her being in the air, just that she needed cooling down, but I can see how it would have looked. Thank you for explaining everything to me. You can have your wards put back up or not, but please don't be afraid of me. I would never cause you harm. You provided for me and kept me clean, fed and safe. For that I thank you. But, I won't visit again."

"No," my mum protested. "We want to see you. Now you know and we can openly protect ourselves. You're still our daughter."

My dad interrupted. "You need time to process everything and I know a relationship with us would take time under the circumstances. But Polly would like to get to know you. She doesn't know about magic and we're not sure how to deal with that. Maybe we can talk it over some other time. When did your magic return?"

"This last week. I didn't know what was happening to me. I started having dreams in which someone who said she was my real mum appeared. She looks like you described but as you can imagine, I'm having a hard time processing that any of this is real."

"It will take a long time to adjust. It did us," my dad answered.

"Well, thank you for meeting with me," I said. "Oh, just one thing. Do you still have the number my mum gave you?"

My dad nodded and went in his pocket. "I thought you'd ask for it."

We said our goodbyes. My leaving was awkward. I didn't want to hug them. With everything they'd said I didn't know what I thought about my relationship with them. I needed some time to process everything. But first I wanted to know if this man could meet me and provide me with further answers.

Once I was en route to the train station I called the landline number I'd been given.

A woman's computerised voice announced, "This number is no longer available. Connecting you to an alternative number unless you say cancel."

I waited.

"Frankie Love speaking."

"You! You knew I had magic, and you stopped it. Oh, you certainly have some explaining to do," I told him. "Get ready, I'm on my way back to my house. I'll be there at eleven. Meet me."

"I'm already there. Wizards have no problems with locks. By the way, you need to get some beers in. I've magicked some up, but that doesn't help local businesses."

Ending the call, I walked towards the train station. I'd come looking for answers and ended up with more questions than ever.

Chapter Twelve

Theo

Great, I finally get the woman of my dreams and she thinks I'm attacking her friend the one night she can't meet me. A complete and utter lack of trust. Okay, she's only known me for a week and I have confessed in writing to draining my family of their blood, but I was a fledgling then. It's not my fault my sire was killed. If he'd have survived, I'd have been prevented from the thirst. He would have taken me to a blood bank. I called Reuben and Darius and asked if they fancied a drink at mine. Reuben and myself were enjoying a nice vintage of blood and Darius loved scotch, so I'd given him a bottle. Rav was working so he couldn't join us.

"So, what's this all about? We don't usually see you more than once a week. What's happened to your elusive vampire side?" asked Reuben.

"Women," I said.

Darius spluttered scotch down his cream cashmere jumper. "Fuck. That'll have to go in the bin. Cashmere doesn't clean well."

"I'll buy you a new one," I grumbled. "What's another fuck up today?"

"Hell, you are down in the dumps," declared Reuben, looking at Darius' jumper. "Bloody hell, Darius, what a mess. You weres are so uncouth. You need a bib."

"Hilarious. Don't go for stand-up any time soon," Darius snarled.

Reuben flashed his eyes red at him.

"Yeah, yeah, yeah. Vamp party trick. They don't look as good as mine," Darius said and flashed his wolf eyes with their hint of yellow.

"You two. Real problems here." I called their attention back to me. "Shelley thinks I took a bite out of her friend."

"What?" Reuben laughed. "Nice one. How did she come to that conclusion? Her friend's dating that dodgy magician, right? Whatever happened to her, you can bet he'll be responsible."

"My tie was left at the scene."

"Couldn't the magician have conjured one up?" said Darius.

I sat back. That made a lot of sense. "Yes. Yes, you're right, he could. It'll be Mr Turnip trying to cause trouble. He's started giving Shelley lessons in magic. He's trying to drive a wedge between us. I know it."

"Magic?" Said Reuben. "Why would Shelley be having lessons in magic? She's mortal, isn't she?"

"Yes, well, it appears not. She's apparently half-witch on her mother's side. Human father."

"Really? How interesting. So how did she find that out?"

"Every time she's been losing her temper, some object has gone flying, apparently. She coated me in coca-cola on our date. I just thought she'd spilled something."

Reuben guffawed. "Her magical powers are spilling coca-cola? Gosh, let's all hide."

"Yeah, well she was going to visit her adoptive parents tonight to try to get some answers on her background. I don't know if this is the extent of her powers or if they'll get stronger. I might not get to find out if she bins me off thinking I've had a drink of her best friend."

"Bin you off? What sort of language is that?" said Reuben.

"Modern language, you old bastard," replied Darius. "It means to terminate the relationship."

"I'll terminate you if you don't show some respect to your superior."

"Stop it, you two. For goodness sake," I told them. "Can we have one night without your sparring?"

Darius looked at Reuben. "He really is a misery guts, isn't he? Put it there, bro." They bumped fists.

"So, what do I do?" I asked them both.

"Take her out on a nice date. Go into the country or something with a picnic. Women like that kind of thing, and suggest she avoids Frankie. He's up to something. I will keep an eye on him, see what he does while you're both out."

"You'd do that for me? Thank you."

"You're my best friend," said Reuben, "and seeing as how Darius is a cop, he can help me."

"Yeah, I can cover the day shift, you mean." Darius rolled his eyes.

"Are you making fun of my disability? Sleep impairment is no laughing matter."

"You're not sleep impaired, you're undead, you cretin," yelled Darius.

They proceeded to carry on bickering and I sat back, enjoying my drink and left them to it. I felt better now we had a plan.

Now to convince Shelley that the only person I wanted to bite was her.

Chapter Thirteen

Shelley

"Why didn't you tell me the whole truth?" I snapped at Frankie.

"Because it was your adoptive parents place to tell you, not mine. Now we can move forward because you can know the rest of the story."

"There's more?"

"Of course. Don't you wonder why your real mother can only appear to you in a dream?"

"She told me. Because of Lucy."

"Ah, yes, Lucy." He sat back on my sofa. "Go get us a bottle of wine to share, dear. I think we'll need it."

I stood up to head to the kitchen. "I thought you bought beer?"

"I've already drunk those."

"How old are you, anyway?"

"Thirty-seven, why?"

I shrugged. "I wondered if wizards lived for hundreds of years like vampires."

"'Fraid not, though you can anti-age your wrinkles and give yourself a different look entirely. He waved a hand over his face so it looked like Prince William was sitting on my sofa. It wavered off. "It doesn't stay very long though, a day at the most, so I don't tend to bother with it."

"You were only young then when my parents asked for your help."

"Yes, but I'm a very strong wizard. Always have been."

"Oh, right By the way, do you really like my friend?" I asked him. "Or have you been dating her to keep an eye on me?"

"I do like her, but Kim and I are frankly, what you call, fuck buddies. Neither of us sees a future in it and there'll be no hard feelings when we're done. In fact, the minute I stop going hard, I'll call it quits."

I made a vomiting noise. "You're gross."

"What can I say, she loves the wand." He sighed. "Now, what do you have to do to get a drink around here?"

"Okay." Frank took a drink of wine. "So, before she became a demon, Lucy dated your father – your real father."

He gazed out of the window. "They were engaged

to be married, the church was booked, and then your mother moved to Withernsea."

"She stole him?" I gasped.

"It was more of a case of love at first sight. Your father was torn. He visited the boutique, which at that time was run by Ebony's mother, who was also a seer. She told him that he was meant to be with your mother. That they would have a child. He ended his relationship with Lucy and called off the wedding."

I put a hand over my mouth while I considered what he'd just said. "She must have been devastated. To lose someone she loved and for it to happen in the place where she lived."

"She was furious, swore to get revenge against them. Ebony's mother, Yolanda, allowed them to stay in the apartment over the boutique."

"My business premises?" I queried.

"Yes. One night a fire started. Your parents escaped. Yolanda wasn't so lucky and neither was Lucy."

"She killed Yolanda? And then what, got trapped or died of smoke inhalation?"

"She denied having set the fire as she was taken out on the stretcher, but the next we knew, Lucy appeared in Hell, having become a devil and taking the post of head of Hell."

"A devil, not *the* Devil?"

"No, you are thinking of Satan himself. He oversees

Hell and has his subjects to guard his empire. Lucy became one of them, and she took your father with her. We don't know how she did it. It has never been known for a human to cross the planes without death, and indeed, to go to Hell without committing an evil deed. Your mum went into hiding until you were born but eventually went to the astral plane, meaning she had no earthly body for Lucy to capture or torture, but she could still communicate and try to find a way to rescue your father. She has yet to be successful, but that is why she is able to communicate with you via your dreams."

I drank down a whole glass of wine. "Well, if I didn't think things were complicated before. Now I discover I have Hell and an astral plane to deal with."

"There are many planes of existence, but for now we need to talk about those that are currently relevant."

"Well, Lucy is angry with me because I'm trying to make Withernsea happy and in love. She doesn't know who I am yet. There'd have been more than a hanging flame warning, I'm sure, if she knew who I really was."

"It won't be long before she works out the truth. Now, we need to develop your magic as we don't know what her next move will be. You are powerful, Shelley, more powerful than a half-witch is supposed to be, and I have no explanation for that. However, I have been letting your magic out a little at a time so you can embrace it rather than be overwhelmed. I believe you are much more powerful than I am, and that is why we must tread carefully."

"You've been putting the brakes on my magic?"

"Yes."

"I healed bite wounds on Kim this morning."

"Bite wounds? She didn't mention this to me?" Frank looked concerned.

"Because she didn't know what they were. She thought they were insect bites and once I'd healed them, she probably thought no more about it. She also found Theo's tie at her bedside."

"Hmm." Frank scratched his chin. "And what do you make of that?"

"Well I asked Theo outright. He wasn't very impressed."

"I should imagine not."

"You don't think he did it?"

"I can't say whether he did or didn't. I don't know him that well, which is why I told you to be careful. But he's 126-years-old, surely leaving a tie by a bedside would be a little careless?"

I placed my hand over my eyes and took a deep breath before letting my hand fall back to my lap. "I accused him. Shit. No wonder he was mad at me. What am I going to do next?"

"I'm going to teach you two things tonight. Firstly, how to see through glamour, as you didn't need to see those cobwebs you told me about. You'll be able to recognise that things like the hanging flame aren't real too. Then I'm going to teach you how to make your own glamour. They can come in very useful. Tomorrow, as its plain to see how desperate you are to see that vampire again, why don't you spend the day with him, give him the benefit of the doubt and practice your glamour on him? It could be fun."

"Thanks, Frankie, for everything." I hugged him. "A day out where I can try to figure things through sounds like a good idea."

I called Theo and apologised for my earlier behaviour. He still wanted to visit the farm, so I agreed we'd go there the next day. I called Kim and told her I was taking the day off and that she'd better do some work if she was there alone. I was busy working on my glamour, to see if it was possible to make Theo look like someone else for a short while and get him past the doorway of the farmhouse. All I had to do was contact the estate agents in the morning. I couldn't see it being a problem since the farm had been on the market for years.

Then I settled myself down to sleep. It had been a long and exhausting day. I should have known that I'd have a visit the minute I dropped off.

"Shelley."

"Oh, for goodness sake. I need my sleep. I've got to have my wits about me tomorrow."

My mum was sitting on a magic carpet that hovered midair. "But you believe it now? That I'm your mum?"

"Yes. Well done. You're no longer the strangest thing in my life."

"I'm glad Frankie is teaching you how to use your magic. I can feel it in you now. It's getting stronger. You need to gain your strength so I can come back and we can fight Lucy for your father."

"YOU WANT ME TO FIGHT A DEVIL. ARE YOU OUT OF YOUR MIND?"

"You need to harness that temper. It will come in handy when we face her."

"Can I go back to sleep now? This is not what I need to hear when I'm trying to relax and figure out my life."

"Well I'm sorry that I'd like to come back to earth and be in my body and reunite with your father. We'd quite like to be a family unit with our daughter, you know."

"Hmmm, I wonder if my magic can push you out of my mind when I'm not in the mood? We'll speak soon, Mum, but I've had enough for one day."

"Shelley, that's so rude."

psychic push

Hey it worked. Now I can go back to sleep.

It was only a ten-minute drive to Goodacre's Farm. As soon as I got in the car alongside Theo, I wished we weren't going anywhere except for my bedroom. I craved him like he must surely crave blood. I'd deliberately not done any magic, so that I didn't smell, but as we started to approach the Withernsea countryside a strong smell of manure worked its way through the car vents.

"Jesus. I forget how bad that smell can be." I pulled a face.

Theo looked at me, opened his mouth to say something and then looked away.

"What?"

"Nothing."

"Out with it, vampire. What were you going to say?"

"Just that this is how you smell to me when you've done magic."

My jaw dropped. *I smelled like this manure farm smell?*

"Times about twenty."

I smelled even WORSE than this farm smell?

I took my mobile phone out of my bag and dialled Frank.

"Dude. I smell like turnips to my boyfriend. Can I switch that off?"

The sound of laughter came down the phone. "It's fun watching those superior little noses turn up in disgust."

"Not when you're dating one."

He huffed. "Fine. It's easy to turn off. You just have to eat a slug every morning."

"Ewwww. I have to what? You've got to be kidding me. I wretch every time I watch *I'm A Celebrity*."

Guffaws came down the line again. "God, you're easy to wind up. Just have a mouthful of rosehip tea every morning and you won't smell to the vampire. If he pisses you off don't drink it and perform a series of spells. He might even be sick. That's such fun."

I heard a door creak and Kim's voice in the background.

"Who are you talking to, Frankie?"

"Gotta go," he said and ended the call.

Theo sighed. "How well do you know this wizard?"

I brought him up to date with everything that had happened. "So you see, he knew my mum, so that makes me trust him. Well, as much as I trust anyone right now."

"Yes, about that. Do you still believe I bit your friend?"

I lay a hand across my breastbone. "No. I'm sorry, Theo. I panicked. You're my boyfriend but she's been my assistant and best friend for a long time. I don't want anything to happen to her."

"That's understandable, but you have my solemn vow that the only person I intend to bite is you."

My betraying core went slick at his words. *For God's sake have some control down there.*

As we approached the long winding driveway of the farm, Theo stopped the car. "Go on then, get this over with."

"Okay, you need to be completely quiet. I've only had the tiniest bit of practice."

He closed his eyes and sat preternaturally still. Show off undead bastard. I closed my eyes and concentrated on conducting a glamour to make him look different.

The trouble was that every time I closed my eyes all I could think about was his cock. I opened one eye and sure enough his head was a giant penis.

Oh my fucking God. Please don't stay like that.

"I'm tingling, is this working now? Only I'm not sure I can cope with the smell much longer."

"No. Be quiet or it'll go wrong and you'll look like a dick," I said. Not telling him how true my words were.

I needed to think of someone I didn't find attractive quickly so I'd stop thinking of cock. I closed my eyes and imagined Simon Cowell. Good, now I'd calmed my libido down I could fashion a normal face for Theo. Except, I couldn't. Every time I opened my eyes he was still Simon Cowell. Oh fuck.

"Er, Theo." I told him. "There's a slight hiccup."

When Jim Gilbert opened the door to his house viewers, his face paled, and he stood there in complete shock. "S-S-Simon?"

I stood forward and shook his hand. "Yes. I must ask you to not tell anyone about this visit to your property. It's highly confidential. Mr Cowell needs somewhere remote where he can escape his legion of fans and your farm looks ideal."

"Oh, of course. Of course. Please, come in," Jim said. "Can I get you a drink? I have tea, coffee, and I know it's early but I have a really special whiskey I was bought for my 40th birthday that we could open." He looked at Theo, who said nothing. Of course, he couldn't because he didn't sound like Simon Cowell.

"Mr Cowell prefers not to speak and to let me handle everything for him," I said. "A drink will not be necessary, but thank you. Could you show us around please?"

"Of course. I'll give you a brief tour and then I'll let you walk around by yourselves."

"That would be fantastic. If anyone asks you met with Shelley Linley and Bob Landry."

"Landry. God, don't mention that name to me," Jim said. "I know a freaking nutcase with that name."

I saw Theo's body stiffen.

"Well, we're short on time, so if we could move things along?" I said.

"Sure."

Once Jim had shown us around, he left us to look around ourselves. Now I could see through glamour, I could switch my sight and see Theo, but poor Jim must have shit a brick when he'd opened his door.

"The farm has been modernised since I was here. There's barely a trace of my old home left."

"Does that mean you can leave it behind? Move on?"

"I don't know. It is rooted in my origins. I was born here, and I died here."

"But don't you have bad memories of your family dying here?"

"I have more good memories. It could be a happy place again. My childhood was extremely happy. We could raise our babies here?"

I looked at him. "Forgetting the fact that we've been dating a week, if we did have a baby, how does it age? Also, how can it have a brother or sister if you're only fertile every hundred and one years?"

"We'd likely only have one. There's no knowing when a vampire will stop aging. It could be in childhood or adulthood. I was turned at twenty-six and aged a little more."

"When will you turn me?"

"When you ask me to."

"What if I carry on aging until my sixties or even older? I'll look like a cougar?"

"Then I'd see if Ebony had a makeup set that could make me look the same age."

"You were looking for a vampire wife when you applied to my agency. Wouldn't that be easier for you?"

"I was only looking for a vampire wife because I hadn't met you." He leaned over and kissed me. Unfortunately in my surprise I dropped my magic and so it was Simon Cowell who gave me a kiss. Jesus Christ.

Theo led me into an empty barn packed with fresh hay. "Ever made love outside?" he asked.

"No!" I answered, "and I'm not about to start right now. What if Jim comes in and sees Simon plugging his assistant? He could sell that story to a news channel."

"Dearest, Shelley." Theo stroked down my cheek. "There's a bolt on the barn door."

"What about security cameras?"

"I'm a technical genius remember? Trust me. We're all alone."

"But I smell bad."

"I want you too much to care."

"Gee, thanks. I think."

Then he leaned over and kissed my neck. My total weak spot. Goose bumps erupted across my skin. I closed my eyes so the Mr Cowell look-alike remained at bay. Theo backed me onto some hay bales. Unlike in the movies, it was actually quite scratchy, but he really seemed to dig it here so I didn't try to conjure up a bed or a blanket. Anyway, I'd probably make the hay bale into another giant penis with how my mind was focusing on Theo's right now. Theo unbuttoned his trousers, lowering those and his boxers and slipped my pants to my knees. Then he nudged into me making me gasp.

But I couldn't help it. I started scratching my arse cheeks. The hay was unbearably itchy. As I began to writhe beneath him, Theo took it as my ecstasy and pounded into me, meaning that the hay scratched my butt even more.

"Arrgh. Stop. Stop right now," I shouted.

Theo opened his eyes. "Sorry. Is there a problem?"

"Yes. I just had anal with a few pieces of straw and my arse is being scratched to death. We need to stop. I'm sorry but this just isn't sexy."

Theo gathered me up and turned me over so that I was on my feet, resting my hands on the hay bale instead. He lowered himself down and licked all across my ass cheeks. I felt my skin tingle.

"All gone," he said. "Vampire venom at its finest."

I touched my butt cheeks. He was right. I couldn't feel a thing.

"Thank you." I said. "Sorry about us not, you know, doing it."

Theo's tongue began again, this time trailing from my butt cheek and down between my thighs.

"Who said we're not doing it?" he said before plunging his tongue inside me.

"Oh my God, Theo. Don't stop." I told him. He brought me to the brink before taking me from behind. Once again, he bit my neck as I came, making my knees give way as thunderous, multiple orgasms crashed through me. He pulled up my pants and gathered me into his arms.

"Please, Theo. Buy the farm. Pay the money. We can chase down your sire's sire later. You need to buy this place. I can see what it means to you," I told him.

"You just want to have outdoor sex again." Theo grinned.

"I can buy thick blankets. Think about how many places we've not done it yet."

Theo sighed. "If I transfer the money to you, will you purchase it? Then I've kept my solemn vow that I would not buy back my farm. It will be in your name instead."

"Theo."

"Once I have the money back from my sire's sire, you can transfer the property to joint names, as married couples are advised these days."

"Theo, I am not your wife," I told him.

"But you will be. Why fight it, Shelley? You know you're never going to want another man's cock as long as you live. You're addicted to mine. My one hundred and ten years of experience is not going to be matched."

"Huh, conceited much? What gave you that impression?"

"The fact your hand is currently stroking the top of my trousers."

Oh, shit. It really was. This was becoming quite a habit.

Chapter Fourteen

Shelley

I seriously had no idea how to find Theo's sire's sire. It's not like there was a Vampires Reunited and he's already tried Faceblood, putting out a random status about anyone who might have been in the area of Goodacre's Farm in August 1907. Theo didn't even know the sire's name. Anyway, I had lots of work to do today. Membership applications were coming in thick and fast. As I noted how many of them stated their supernatural status, I realised that my best friend was going to have to be brought into the fold.

I buzzed through to her office. "Kim, you got a sec?"

"Yeah," she said. She sounded like she had a cold. I wondered if my healing would work on that.

Kim pushed open my door. Her eyes were puffy and she'd obviously been crying.

"Oh my God, Kim. Is everything okay? I thought it was strange you'd not said hello this morning."

"Are you sleeping with Frankie?" she yelled.

I threw my head back. "What? Of course not. Whatever gave you that idea?"

"Well, I went into the bedroom yesterday morning and he was on the phone. I heard a woman's voice coming from the speaker. He rang off quickly and when I asked him who it was he said it was no one important. When he went to the bathroom, I looked at his phone and the call was from you. He's saved you on his phone as Spelly Shelley-he's given you a pet name and everything. How could you?" She burst into noisy sobs again.

"Kim. I am not sleeping with Frankie. Ugh. I am however shagging Theo and enjoying it very much. Now, I'm getting the emergency wine out of my drawer because I need to bring you up to date with something and when I do, you'll probably want to drink the entire bottle."

"Oh my God, is Frankie dying?" Kim wailed. "Did he confide in you? Does he need a kidney? I can give him a kidney."

For her own good I walked over and slapped her face. "Sorry about that, but you need to focus."

She rubbed her face. "You hit me! You cow! This had better be good or I'm going to bitch slap you right back."

I patted her arm. "There's no easy way to say this so I'm going to go for it like pulling a plaster off really quickly. I've discovered I'm half-witch, Theo is a vampire, and Frankie is a wizard."

"Well, it's cool you telling me what you're dressing as for Halloween, but can you get to the fucking point?" Kim rolled her eyes.

"No, Kim. We *really* are those things."

"Fuck off. You're not funny."

I concentrated and put a glamour on the wine bottle, making it look like it was hanging in midair and pouring over the office floor. Kim quickly held her glass underneath it, her face contorting, trying to work out how it was in midair and how her glass wasn't filling with liquid. I took the glamour away.

"What the fuckety fuck?"

"I'm a half-witch. My mother was a witch. Half of Withernsea are supernatural beings. I don't know how many species but apparently werewolves are a real thing too."

Ebony bolted through the door just after Kim fell sideways off her chair. She grabbed Kim and the glass. "I saw this in a flash vision. Sorry I kind of broke your door. She gets it and it won't take her long, don't worry."

"She does? She'll be okay about it?"

"It's Kim. You'll wish you'd not told her. You need to phone Frankie because in an hour she's going to call him and ask if he can magic an even bigger dick for her pleasure."

Sure enough, when Kim came to and had another ten minutes or so of asking me ridiculous questions like whether I could teleport Orlando Bloom into the office, (No. I may have tried. Don't judge me. We'd have sent him back with his memory wiped-joking!), she's beyond excited that her 'drab world has suddenly become technicolour'.

"Well, there's a large reason why I wanted to share this information with you. Regardless of the fact you're my best friend, you're also my assistant and we are becoming overrun with new membership requests from our supe friends. So, I'm opening another wing of Withernsea Dating - the Supernatural Dating Agency. Totally off-grid, we interview our new members and place them under this agency. I've asked Theo, and he's going to alter our computer systems so if we're audited, only the humans appear. However, under the new agency, we can matchmake supes with other supes. I'm not sure how we'll progress if they want a human date, but let's take that as it comes."

"Maybe a legal disclaimer that they won't eat their date, or hex them if they don't like them?"

"Like I said, we have a lot to think about as we start our latest venture."

"I can't wait," said Kim.

"Kim, you realise you're not a member, right?"

"Yeeeeesss."

"You can't like ask them to strip or anything. Or send a nude photo with their application.

"God, you spoil all my fun."

"You were crying earlier because you thought I'd stolen your boyfriend."

"No, I wasn't."

"Erm, excuse me, you had snot running down your nose. It was gross."

"That was because I thought he'd ruined my friendship with you. Frankie is just a fuck buddy. He's not the love of my life. We know where we're at with things. Now, I have a whole new world to explore. He can give me the magic goods and I can still look around. What's happening with you and Theo, anyway? Is it going well?"

"He's giving me £430,000 to buy his old family farm until we can find his sire-long story-and then we'll own it together because it's going to be our marital home and we'll bring up our children there, apparently."

"Oh my God, Shelley. That's a bit heavy. Shall we run off with the money and fly to Rodeo Drive?"

"The stupid thing is that I actually believe this is all going to happen." I sat back in my chair, only just realising this was how I was feeling. "It's like a gut instinct. Like everything is happening exactly how it should."

"I can't believe your mum comes to you in dreams

and you can shut her out. Can you put my mum in one? She does my head in."

BOOOOOOOOOOOOMMMMMMMM. The noise was accompanied by an explosion of glass and the smell of smoke as my office curtains set on fire. I looked at Kim and realised we were within a protective shield that looked like a giant blown bubble. I pressed against it and it felt spongy.

"Right, let me concentrate and get us out of here," I told Kim, whose eyes were wide. I slowly got us to the door and out into the hall. The bubble disintegrated and we ran like hell for the fire exit.

Everyone from the shops and offices was gathered outside. Jax ran over to us as we emerged. "Thank God. Are you alright? The fire brigade and the police are on their way."

"Yeah," I said but I was everything but alright. Especially when I looked at the back of the crowd and saw the woman who was in Jax's coffee shop that time before our meeting. She looked directly at me, flicked her fingers and a little flame danced on the top of one of them. Was this Lucy? I tried to push my way through the crowd, Kim hot on my heels, but she was nowhere to be seen. It was like she'd just vanished into thin air, which I bet she had.

How was I meant to deal with Lucy if I couldn't get near enough to talk to her? Then the police and fire brigade arrived and the afternoon was taken up with crime reports.

My office just needed a little redecoration and as Jax's older brother was a plasterer, painter, and decorator, he promised to fix things up the following week. For the time being I'd have to share Kim's office or take my laptop down to Jax's. I refused to be bullied out of my building.

We were sat in Kim's office shortly before five when a knock came at the outer door. I put the door on the latch and asked who was there.

"It's the police," the man said out loud, and then his voice dropped to a whisper, "The special division."

I let him in. "Are you Shelley Linley?" he asked.

"I am. And you are?"

"Police Constable Darius Wild." He whispered again, "Werewolf."

"Oh," I said, not being able to help myself from giving him a once over. My subconscious, no doubt, looking for fur and claws. All I saw was a good looking man with shaggy brown hair and a beard.

"Ebony's been keeping me in the loop and what happened today came up on our feed. Thought there might be something otherworldly to it. Best to check."

"Come through. We're working in my assistant's

office at the moment." I walked in with him and heard Kim yell out, "Holy fuck."

She quickly covered her mouth. "Sorry, she said. I have the hiccups."

But Darius didn't reply because he was frozen in place, staring at Kim, who was staring right back at him.

"Well, Darius. Would you like to look at the crime scene?" I asked.

He shook himself, coming back to the land of the living. "Oh, yeah, sure." Then he followed me to my office with its scorch marks and soaked through interior.

"I've picked up all the details from the scene of crime officers, but sometimes we can pick up other things, extra clues, like signs of magic etc." He looked around and then walked over to one of the scorch marks. He muttered an incantation and it lit up with a dark red glow. "Yep, that's hellfire."

I sighed. "I've been told I've upset Lucy Fir."

"Oh dear," Darius said. "That's one woman you don't want to get on the bad side of."

"How am I supposed to reason with her if she's in Hell? I'm not going there." I described the woman I saw in the coffee shop before and in the crowd today.

"Yeah, that sounds like Lucy. She doesn't get to come away from her post very often, not unless Satan says so. You must have really upset them."

"Apparently my agency is making Withernsea too happy and loved up. Oh, and my parents have a long-standing feud with Lucy. She kidnapped my dad." I told him everything I knew.

"Ah."

"But how do I stop her?"

"And Satan. Chances are she's acting on his behalf. You have to offer them something they want in return for leaving you in peace. I'm afraid that's how it works. They're not going to bargain for the greater good, so you're going to have to think of something they want that's bad."

"Seriously?"

"I'm afraid so. Now, if we need to get a message to hell it's fine, because Rav is a demon and he can visit there."

"Do you think we could bribe them with a good curry?"

"I wish. Well, I'll leave you to have a think about it. I'll find out when you have the all clear to get this mess fixed up."

"Thank you, that would be appreciated."

"So, what has Theo said about what's happened?"

"You know Theo?"

"Yeah, he's one of my mates."

"Right, well, I kind of haven't told him yet."

Darius chuckled. "I'd love to be a fly on the wall when you do."

He followed me back into the office where another staring session followed between him and Kim. Jesus, was Derren Brown hiding in the cupboard? "Darius? Is that all?"

"Oh, yes. Well, and just to say that I sent in an application for the agency. I'm young, free and single. Well, I'm not free on a full moon, but the rest of the time."

"Ah, yes. We're just updating the service so it'll be even better and we'll be in touch soon," I told him.

"Right, okay. Well, I'll be seeing you."

Kim nodded her head, seemingly unable to speak.

I escorted him out of the office before they could start mooning at each other again.

When I got back Kim was tapping away on her keyboard.

"So, what was that all about? I felt like a third wheel."

"Sorry, I don't know what you're talking about. I'm dating Frankie, remember?" Kim said, going back to her screen.

"Okay then. Well, let's call it a night. I think we've had quite a day."

"Sure," Kim said. As I stood to get my coat, I saw her hastily click away from Darius' application form, recognisable from the photo on the screen. I decided it was better not to mention it.

"I will not allow you to reside by yourself any

longer. I need to protect you through my waking hours and well, if you will let me turn you then you will be protected in my vault during the light."

"No. And you can stop with that manly protector shit. I can look after myself."

"But this is my role. To fight for your honour. I'm not sure how I could duel with a devil. I am entirely sure I would be dust in seconds, but at least I would have tried."

"Listen, I'd like my husband in my bed, rather than in a vase on the mantlepiece."

He grinned, a great beaming smile. "You said husband."

"What can I say? You're growing on me." I winked.

"I am growing right now, actually," he told me, and that was the end of the conversation.

Of course, the next morning when I woke he was gone. It was going to take some getting used to, being the girlfriend and potential wife of a vampire, and whether I wanted to be made undead, I still wasn't sure. What would happen to my witch powers? Then I remembered that I had a devil out to hurt me and the other things faded into insignificance.

"You don't need to send Rav to hell. Lucy comes to every Halloween celebration. She gets to be herself but the people around her obviously don't know her horns are real," Frankie told me.

"So what does she get out of coming here?" I asked him, "other than being able to walk around without a disguise?"

"Well, that in itself is a major part of it, but also she has a quota for Halloween."

"A quota?"

"Midnight is the time when the veil drops and she gets to choose one person. They have to have done something evil to be chosen. But she can go to their house and trick or treat them. Whatever they answer she can show them her true face. She touches them, and they burn from the inside out, then she escorts them to Hell."

"Please tell me being bad isn't running a red light or I've fucked it," I replied.

He chuckled. "No. Murder, child molestation. The kind of stuff that you think ah, well, one less monster to worry about. It's sometimes a shock to see who goes. Last year it was my dog walker. Apparently, some of his charges never made it back to their owners."

"So in a way, she got to protect the animals. Aww bless," I said.

"Shelley—" Frank yelled as a red-hot pointed arrow shot through the window and spiked through Frank's wall. He froze it with water and it fell to the floor with a crash.

"What the hell just happened?" I asked, shaking.

"Hell, just happened." He raised his voice. "You just said 'aww, bless,' about a devil. Are you insane?"

"So, that's a no-no then, saying holy-type words?" I queried.

"If you want to live, I'd steer clear."

"Cool trick there with the ice. I can do that when I'm sent fire?"

"You can learn but you can only control small amounts. No one has the capacity to stop hellfire but Satan, as far as I'm aware, not even the Lord himself. That's kind of the deal between good and evil. They have to keep a kind of truce between the good stuff and the bad stuff. That's why sometimes shit happens, like earthquakes or tsunamis. Some people have to die so that others can live a good life. It's the balance."

"Shit, this stuff is deep. Anyway, so I can get to meet Lucy at the Halloween party down on the beach front?"

"If you can recognise her amongst the other devils, yes."

"Can I not do some kind of location spell?"

Frankie shook his head. "I'm afraid not. Only top-level witches can do location spells and you're only a half-witch. I would love to be able to do them. They could be so helpful."

"Damn. It would be a lot easier if I could just, for instance, wave at the wall and a map would appear and tell me where, like Theo is." I waved my hand, sighed, and rolled back against Frankie's sofa. "This whole thing sucks."

"Wha-..." Frankie coughed.

"Have you got a crisp stuck in your throat again? How many times have I told you about eating too fast?" I sat up. Frankie was staring at the wall where above his television was a drawing of Theo's house and an X. "I thought you said I couldn't do it?"

"Y-y-you shouldn't be able to. This isn't right."

"Well, I can. Where is Kim?" I said. A word came across the wall. U P S T A I R S. "My best friend is upstairs? Oh my God, have you got her waiting up there?" I pulled a face. "Am I after the event or before it?"

"Before, she's cool. She's watching *Emmerdale*."

I got up to leave. "You're weird. So very weird."

"Says the person who can make maps appear on my wall." He creased his brow. "We need to test your magic again. Something's not adding up. Somehow, you've inherited more from your mother than your father, which is rare, though not impossible. Please be careful, it's very strong. Keep doing those protection spells, and extend the wording to those innocents around you. You don't want them hurt by wild magic." He made some words appear across a piece of paper and handed it to me.

"Thank you," I told him. "Now roll on Halloween."

Chapter Fifteen

Shelley

It was Halloween. We'd called a halt to supernatural matchmaking while we dealt with the issue of Lucy. In the meantime, Kim was adding applications to the new system and interviewing prospective clients-or should I say, she was adding the applications to the computer, interviewing the hot male applicants herself, and leaving the rest to me.

"Erm, not fair," I told her. "Leave some totty for me. I need eye candy too."

"You're getting married. I'm allowed to look at all the hot single guys."

"I am not getting married!"

"That's not what Ebony says, and she's a seer."

"I wish I'd never told you about the supe world." I sighed. "Has she said anything about you?"

"Just keeps going on about me dating a police officer."

"Oh my God. I remember her saying that in Jax's. It's you and Darius. I bet you're going to date the werewolf."

"I don't think so."

"What have you got against Darius?"

"Well, for a start I'm dating Frankie and for another thing, well, he has better hair than I do. I can't deal with that."

"I swear you were dropped on the head at birth."

"Not possible, my whole head and body are perfectly shaped."

"Come on," I told her. Looking at her attempt at a ghost outfit which was basically a powdered white face and a white bikini. She was going to freeze to death outside. "How are you a ghost?" I asked her.

"I died sunbathing," she said. "Overheated, had a heart attack."

"Every man out there will have a heart attack if they see you like that." I glamoured a white sheet over her body.

She looked down. "Take that off me right now." She tried to grab it but couldn't, seeing as it wasn't real. "This is an outrage. You're using your magic for bad things. Isn't this against some code or something?"

"Let's go." I pulled her by the arm, "and remember

there will be children present in the cafe so no swearing at me."

"I'd better do it now then," she said, letting out a stream of expletives that showed me exactly what she thought of the outfit I'd fashioned for her.

∽

I'd thought Lucy might show up at the cafe open day but she didn't, so it looked like I was going to have to look for her down at the beach. I agreed to meet Kim at The Marine at 7:30pm.

"How will you find me in that crowd?" Kim asked. "You going to use a location spell?"

"No need. I'll look for the most naked person. The one surrounded by narrow-eyed women and men with their tongues hanging out. It shouldn't be difficult."

"So, you're going to take this monstrosity off me then?" she snarked.

"Yes, as soon as you get home, it'll disappear."

"Thank God for that."

"Look, you have to admit that when the local church's under-six choir walked in, you were pleased to be dressed."

"Yeah, whatever. Right, see you at The Marine. Are you staying dressed like that?" She pointed to my female vampire outfit which Theo had told me to save for later.

"Nope. I'm going as myself. Well, half of myself," I told her.

I figured if I was half-witch I needed to embrace it, so I'd bought a long dark wig and a pointy hat, plus a witch's costume. I looked pretty cute if I said so myself.

~

Theo came to pick me up dressed as a werewolf, complete with Wolverine type fingers. We'd seen each other every night since we visited the farm, apart from Thursdays when he had a card night with his friends. I used that night to rest from all the sexual marathons we kept having.

"So, I guess I'll see Darius as a vampire?"

"You got it. We like to... what do you call it, 'take the piss' out of each other on Halloween."

We drove down to The Marine and met up with Kim who was standing next to Frankie. Kim was dressed as a corpse bride.

"Nice outfit," I said to her rather angry looking face.

"Well, I was dressed in my ghost sunbather costume but another of the magical crew decided to dress me in another outfit." She gave Frankie a stink eye.

"Too many people were staring. I was at risk of turning them into snakes. It was easier to conjure you an outfit. In any case, you look even more sensational and will probably win outfit of the night."

"That's true. I do look amazing." She twirled. "Not like what *she* dressed me in earlier."

"Well, as fun as this is. I need to search for Lucy. Text me if you see her and remember our plan."

"You're not going alone," Theo said. "I'm coming with you."

"And me," said Kim.

"And me," added Frankie.

"Come on then," I said. "Let's get this over with."

"You don't smell of turnips this evening," Theo said to Frankie.

"Theo!"

"It's fine. I took something so you could avoid the odour. I'm nice like that. Whereas I'm failing to see any endearing qualities in your undead self." Frankie looked Theo up and down.

"I know, let's split up into two teams. I'm sure that would be more effective. Now, do you have your mobiles on in case we need to contact you?" I said.

"We can communicate telepathically. Try it now. Just think of me and say help," said Frankie. I closed my eyes and imagined Lucy trying to set me on fire.

"What are you doing to him?" Kim screamed.

I opened my eyes. Kim told me Frankie had been buzzing.

"It's fine. I'll know to ask to manifest to wherever

Shelley is," he said, then he and Kim went off in another direction.

Theo and I walked down the busy promenade and I stared at every devil. I didn't want to do a location spell if I could help it as it might give Lucy a signal that I was looking for her. I didn't know enough about how it worked. Music started up, and the crowds began to thicken. It became more difficult to stick together.

And then she was in front of me. Her eyes flashing red as she clutched my arm. She slashed open, what I knew from films, to be a portal to her left and dragged me through it.

I found myself sitting back in my own home.

"Well, well, well. If it isn't Shelley Linley. Or as you were born, Michelle Cast. I thought it was annoying enough that you were here in Withernsea upsetting Satan by creating love unions, but to find that you're the golden child, well, that was just the rain on my bonfire and I don't like it damp."

"How did you find out it was me?"

"Because my boss hangs around Withernsea. He got all the gossip from dear Theo."

Theo. Satan knows Theo? What the actual fuck?
"What do you want, Lucy?"

She looked at her blood-red pointed talons. "I ended up in Hell because of your parents, so I kinda think you can't offer me much in the way of a deal. Whereas I can play with you and make your life, well,

Hell." She laughed and little flames sparked from her horns-two tiny protrusions atop her head.

I tilted my head as I met her gaze. "I get you were pissed that my dad went off with Mum. I would have been. To be honest, I'm on your side about the whole 'try to split them up thing' because to dump you before your wedding was pretty shit, but how is this my fault? I can't help that I was born."

She sat back on my couch, which was annoying since she kept sparking and singeing the lovely leather.

"I knew Ebony's mother. She'd told me of her prophecy. That your father kept a secret, handed down through the generations. She saw a child, she said, who would be very powerful. She said that child's child would eventually rule all of Withernsea." She shot flames at my candles, lighting them all up. "I thought she meant me. My child. Our child. Mine and Dylan's."

"Oh."

"When your father met your mother, they humiliated me. Yolanda's predictions became clearer though. She said it was your mother that would have the baby."

"So you set the fire and killed Yolanda?"

"No." Lucy's eyes flashed with red and my curtains set fire and dropped to the floor in ashes.

"I stood near their apartment, near the boutique, and wished revenge on them all for their betrayal. Your mother had just announced her pregnancy. A man approached me. He looked like a vampire. He said he could transport me and your father away to a different place if I would agree to work for him. He said he managed people, and it was somewhere hot and away from here. I loved your father, so I agreed. I guessed he had a supernatural connection, most of Withernsea had. Apart from me—I was one of the ordinary people, yet not good enough for your mortal father. I now know where the phrase Hell hath no fury like a woman scorned originates from."

She turned to me and reduced the cushions either side of me to ashes. I tried to raise a protective bubble around myself but that just made her laugh louder.

"I made a deal with the devil." Lucy smiled. "He looked so normal, but he was able to make a deal with me as I had evil intent in my mind. I'd been thinking about your parents, how they didn't deserve happiness, but ruin, and I had thoughts about killing them. Just anger, but that was enough for him to work with. He set fire to the flat, and it spread to the shop."

"The devil?"

"Satan himself. The minute I agreed to the deal strands of red smoke wrapped around me. Your mother and father were caught up in the fire. The Devil grabbed me and dragged me into the flames. They were trying to get out. I told your father that if he wanted to save you and your mother that he had to come with me. He could see I was corrupted by evil but he agreed. Otherwise, all three of you would have perished in that fire. When the fire brigade arrived, I was placed on a stretcher. Your parents walked outside. I thought I'd hallucinated the whole thing, that somehow, I'd been in the fire and it had affected my mind but then I found myself guarding Hell itself. Your father was bound to the same place, but he was there to suffer."

"But how could my father go to Hell if he hadn't made the deal himself?"

"Because when he saw me and realised I was going to split you all up, just for a moment he wished to kill me. His evil intent was enough. Of course, feeling even more bitter and twisted because I now lived in Hell, I told Satan about your mother's pregnancy. But it appears that the ones upstairs argued that Satan had upset the balance by taking your father and so your mother was to be protected.

"So indirectly, Satan actually saved my life?"

"Yes, something he has never forgiven the gods for. Satan has ruled Withernsea for years now, walking around and living there as one of their own, while I tend the fires of Hell for him. While he was happy at the misery in Withernsea, I was left alone. You think I'm the enemy but I'm just a puppet, *Michelle*. Now you're trying to make those he ruins happy, so you need to be taken care of."

"If its Satan that wants to ruin me, why have you kidnapped me?"

"Because you're going to help me escape Hell. Now there's a deal you can offer me. Help me escape and I'll free your father so he and your mother can get back together in Withernsea."

"But I thought you didn't want them together?"

"I've been stuck in one place with him for twenty-six years with no escape. I'm sick of looking at his damn face, or should that be damned face? It's time for a change."

"It doesn't look like I have much of an option, does it?" I told her.

"Not really." She said. "Also, I get to take someone evil with me to Hell on Halloween and if you don't comply, I'll take Theo. He's a murderer after all."

I wanted to call her a bitch, but I knew from dealing with a premenstrual Kim when to keep my mouth shut and this was PMT x 1000 sitting on my sofa. "You said Satan has been walking around the streets amongst everyone for all this time?"

"Yes! He enjoyed taking a bite out of your friend. He wasn't impressed that you managed to heal the wounds. They were supposed to turn your friend evil. She would have begun to kill your other friends off one by one. You've pissed him off. He detects that the prophecy has started. That you have strong powers.

"Run this past me again. Satan's been walking around Withernsea as a vampire?"

"He has. He said tonight he's going to finish off the

job he's started on your friend. He can't come after you directly but he can kill some of your friends until you agree to make a deal with him." She looked at her red nails. "I'll bet he's there right now."

"Take me back," I shouted.

"Do we have a deal?" She smiled slowly.

"Yes. I will help you get out of Hell for the freedom of my parents."

"Excellent. As soon as I'm free, I will free your father."

"Now excuse me a minute while I do a location spell to find my friend," I told her. I stared at the wall and saw she was in a backstreet near the amusements.

"Can you take me there?" I asked Lucy.

"I suppose so," she said, then grabbed me and back we went through a portal.

I appeared in the alleyway, Lucy standing behind me. Kim was lying on the floor.

Laying over her, his mouth on her neck, was Theo.

"Oh my God." I said. "Are you Satan?"

Chapter Sixteen

Shelley

Theo stood up, Kim's blood dripping from his mouth. "Of course I'm not Satan. Have you been drinking? I got a call from Frankie saying they'd been having a drink and Kim didn't feel he was giving her enough attention, so she stomped out of the pub. He gave her a minute and then went after her, but she was nowhere to be seen.

"So how did you find her?"

"She's bleeding. It's like a homing beacon to me. I'm trying to close her wounds with my saliva but it's not working."

"Because they're not vampire wounds. Here, let me." I moved towards Kim.

"Oh my God, what's she doing here?" Theo asked.

"Oh, yeah, Theo - Lucy. Lucy - Theo."

"Pleasure," said Lucy. "By the way, behave yourself or I'm taking you to Hell with me tonight."

I looked at Theo and shook my head. "Not the time to ask right now."

I put my fingers on the bite marks that once again marred Kim's neck and closed my eyes. I felt what appeared like bubbling from underneath and a thick red sticky liquid came out of her mouth, heat making it sizzle.

"Oh my God, what has he done to her?"

I envisaged Kim's body in my mind. I saw red-hot liquid in her system, so I imagined a cool, icy, nitrogen style antidote, the white smoke chasing the hot liquid out of her body. Kim spluttered. Theo held her while she vomited the red liquid again and again. Then she opened her eyes.

"What the fuck?"

I sent the psychic message to Frankie. He materialised in front of me and looked Kim over. "She's okay. She might feel off for a few days, but she'll survive." He looked at me. I nodded.

"But Shelley. I don't know how you're doing this. I released the rest of your powers but to be able to thwart Satan. This is beyond anything anyone in Withernsea has ever known."

"Really?" I turned around to Lucy. "I wonder if I can freeze you. Shall I give it a try?" I raised an eyebrow.

She looked back at me warily and took a step backwards. "Maybe you could. But you made a deal with me and that can't be broken now. Not even by a powerful witch."

"So how do I find Satan?"

"You don't. You wait for him."

"Damn. Okay, while I wait how do I get you free so that I can have my parents back?"

"You have to bargain with the devil himself," she said.

I placed a hand on my hip. "Excuse me? You said nothing about this before."

"I'm a devil, you have to anticipate I'll be devious. I'm a bad guy. Jesus, you need lessons in supes."

"So I agreed to free you to get my parents back, not realising you meant I'd have to take on Satan?"

"That's right, babes."

"And I can't do a location spell?"

"Doubt it."

"You can do location spells?" Theo's face seemed to whirr with thoughts. "I know we're busy looking for the devil but can you do one to find my sire's sire? I'll be able to get my money back if we survive hellfire."

"Sure." I flayed my hands in the air. "Not like I've anything better to do."

"Well, while you're pratting around with that, I'm going to get a gingerbread ghost," said Lucy, stomping off.

I conjured up a picture in the night sky that looked

like I drew it with sparklers. "Where is Theo's sire's sire?" I asked.

"That's my house," said Theo.

"I'm going to try to find Satan," I said, "just because other people can't do it, doesn't mean I can't." I looked in the air and pictured the stereotypical devil with horns. A red-hot light shone in the living room of the map of Theo's home. "That can't be right," I said.

Then the light opened into a flaming red portal and a voice shouted out. "Do come and join me, I've been waiting."

"Don't do it, Shelley. It's a trick," said Theo. "It's got to be."

"But if I don't go to see him I don't get my parents back."

"What's going on?" said Lucy. "I felt myself being summoned."

"Bring them through, Lucy," the voice said again.

"Come on, it's fine." Lucy said.

"She could be lying to you." Theo pointed at Lucy. "She said herself that she lies."

I turned and looked at Lucy. "Not this time. She wants to be free. She knows this is the only way Withernsea is freed from his rule."

"But how has he been ruling? I've not seen any evidence of demonic power."

"He's not been walking around as Satan," Lucy said.

"He's been living as a vampire, shagging around. Every one of his women has ended up in hospital with severe burns. I see it all where I am, but I'm powerless to stop him. Plus, one of them ransacked my flat when I disappeared and stole my Mac cosmetics – she had it coming."

"I'll drive us there," said Theo. "He'll just have to wait. It's only a couple of minutes drive from here."

"Well hurry," said the voice from the portal. "Or your friend Darius will be toast."

"I bet I could teleport with practice," I grumbled.

"Well I offered to take you, don't say I didn't," huffed Lucy.

"It's a couple of minutes up the street for Heaven's sake," said Theo, who had been struggling to get his car started.

A flame leapt out of Lucy's fingers and singed his back seat.

"We're in a petrol car, can you not blow us up?" I shouted.

"He's the one who caused that, saying words about the people upstairs." She folded her arms over herself and mumbled something about Hell being easier than real life.

We got out of the car and followed Theo into his house. As we entered the living room, we found two men playing cards.

"Darius? Reuben? I... I just spoke to, well, never

mind. Er, did I invite you round for a game, I don't remember?" Theo said, his face creased in concern.

"What's going on?" I asked.

"This is Darius, as you already know, and this is my best friend Reuben," Theo explained. "So... I'm a little confused."

"Really, you are so stupid," Lucy said. "I've already told you he's been living as a vampire."

"Say what?" I pointed to Reuben. "Is Reuben really Satan?"

"That's impossible," Theo exploded. "Reuben is my best friend, we play cards every Thursday night."

"Yeah and Monday, Tuesday, Wednesday, Friday, Saturday, Sunday, he's either down in Hell or causing death and mayhem here," added Lucy.

"Lucy, my beautiful assistant. Are you enjoying Halloween? Have you decided who your new plaything will be?"

"Yes." She smiled sweetly. "I'm going to take Theo with me."

"What?" yelled Darius.

"Be quiet, wolf, or I'll be having a nice steak for dinner," snarled Satan.

Darius' face paled. "All those times we've played cards and had banter... you were the devil. I can't believe it."

"And you thought it was wereblood that made me volatile. You're so stupid."

"Is there someone else here?" I asked.

"No, why?"

"Because according to my spell, Theo's sire's sire is here as well."

Satan chuckled and raised a hand. "Oooh, that would be me. Basically, I watched Theo's ridiculously stupid sire get attacked and then his sire, the original Reuben, came along, greedily wanting all the money from the sale of the farm so I kind of tore out his evil undead soul and took over his body. I've had various assistants looking after Hell and in the meantime, I've ruled Withernsea. It's been one of the worst places to live. Diabolical in fact. That is until you came along, Shelley. It was okay while you didn't have any powers and only wanted to match up the poor human saps who live here, but oh no, fate, the arse pain she is, decided to send Theo across your path, awakening your powers. I'm afraid that's not going to work for me. Take him to hell, Lucy."

"I want to make a deal," I told him.

"Halt!" he shouted at Lucy. "It would appear a different option has been thrown my way." He stroked his chin. "I need a moment to ponder this. I don't want to waste the offer of a binding deal." His eyes flashed red. What was it with devils and vampires? Was there a shop somewhere with a deal on red contacts?

"Right. I want you to agree that you will not marry or give birth to this man's child," he said, pointing at

Theo. "Also, that you will not arrange any more dates for supernaturals at your agency. I need my supes depressed. They create more death and destruction that way. Now, what do you want?"

"All I ask is that you let Lucy free of her duties and allow her to come back to earth. She was wronged. She didn't deserve to be placed in Hell. By doing so she will free my father and my mother will come out of exile."

"You're willing to give him up for this?"

"To save my family, yes. I want to know my father and mother." I looked at Theo, tears in my eyes. "I am so, so, sorry, but I have to do this."

Theo looked down at the floor. "I can't believe this. I've lost my best friend and my would-be wife in one night."

"Oh, and by the way, Shelley. How is your friend? She sure did taste nice when I bit her. Even better the second time around. It was easy to get Theo's tie from here. Stupid vampire never locks the door. I hope it didn't cause too much trouble between you and your boyfriend. Not that it matters now." Satan laughed, then stood up and shook my hand. "Deal," he said.

"Deal." I agreed. Red and white ribbons of smoke wrapped around our hands before dissipating.

I looked at Theo as the Devil broke into laughter.

"Now," I said.

Chapter Seventeen

Shelley

It all happened in seconds. The deal was binding and in front of me stood a red reptilian looking man. As he spoke I noticed he did indeed have a forked tongue.

"Well, that concludes business," he said.

"I don't think so." A man walked through the door. He had red hair the same as my own and I instinctively knew that this was my father, even before Lucy said "Dylan". He winked at me. "We kept one more secret from you, daughter." In front of our eyes he transformed into a dragon-like creature. Standing on two legs, he had a dragon's head and wings on his back. His trunk and legs were reptilian, and he had a fishlike tail.

"This can't be true," said Lucy.

"What?" I asked.

"He's a wyvern," she said.

"Well, this has been fun, but I'm out of here," said

Satan. "I need to tell Rav that he's back holding the fort."

"Yes, well, there's been a slight change in plan." A deep voice boomed from the dragon's mouth. "I think you'll find that Withernsea is mine."

I would have expected the devil to try to toast my father alive but instead he stood there with a bemused look on his face. "What are you talking about, lizard?"

"Did you not wonder how you were able to plunder this place unchallenged for the last twenty-six years?" said my father. "My family have held the secret of Withernsea for years. Its real name is Wyvernsea, and it belongs to my family. With every child our line grows stronger as our children are born with even more power. I was born half human and half wyvern but as you can see, the wyvern gene wins out, taking the best from the other half and adapting. I could pass for human when I was far from anything of the sort."

That's when the devil did as I'd expected. He shot fire at my father, who took on an icy tomb and remained unaffected. "Whilst ever I'm in Wyvernsea, I am stronger than you and the gods. It was only the fact you took me by surprise in human form, transporting me to hell before I realised what was happening, that resulted in my imprisonment. Now, thanks to you I'm back, my wife is coming back too, and we can be with our daughter.

"Yet, the prophecy isn't going to come true, boohoo," said Satan. "She made a deal not to marry the vampire."

"I didn't," I said.

He turned to me and his look chilled me to the bone. "You made a deal," he snarled.

"Yes, not to marry him," I said, pointing to Theo. "Or to have his babies."

"Is there something I'm not understanding?" spat Satan.

"Yes," I said, and the glamour fell away, revealing that Theo was in fact Frankie.

"Well, hello again," said Frankie. "Good job I knew all about Theo and you lot from our card games. The only thing I struggled with was his car. He really needs something more modern."

In a fury, the devil struck out and smite him. I watched as my friend and mentor fell to the floor, his body charred. Croaks of pain fell from his lips.

"Frankie, no!" I leapt to his side, placing my hands on his skin and imagined healing him, but all I felt was his terrible pain. I held his hand as my magic pulled away.

"It's okay," he told me. "Ebony said this would happen. That I would sacrifice my life but it would be for the greater good." He coughed. "Listen, tell Kim she was a great shag," he tried to laugh but coughed in earnest. "She wasn't meant for me," he said, and with one final scream of pain, his head fell to the side.

My own rage leapt to the surface. As I turned, my dad grasped hold of my hand. "Get ready, I'm passing on your legacy." An icy sensation surged through my body. My legs formed a lizard-like skin and I grew wings.

"You have all the powers but because you're half-witch, your appearance should be kinder," my dad said, and kissed my cheek.

Satan grabbed Lucy. "I agreed she could stay in Withernsea but I don't remember stating she had to be alive, if we're being persnickety." He tilted his head. "Say bye, Lucy."

I shot out a sluice of icy water from my hand. It covered Satan and froze him in place. Lucy dropped to the floor, and I pulled her behind me. Heat burned through my ice until Satan stood there once more.

"Well. It would appear that for now I shall have to return home. But I'll be working on things while I'm down there. At least my supes will remain miserable now you can't arrange their dates."

"I can't," I told him. "But Kim can, and seeing as I'll be getting married and having wyvern/witch/vampire crossbreed babies, I think I'll probably be quite busy anyway. See yourself out."

Satan turned to Lucy. "I'm not removing your horns, and having spent so much time in hell some of it will still be within you. See if you can find love with those on your head."

He vanished, leaving a trail of fire that didn't touch us but burned through Theo's apartment, reducing everything he owned to ash.

I crouched down next to Frankie's body, and I cried and cried and cried.

"How did you and Frankie do that? I didn't see you swap?" said Lucy.

"We did it when you bought your gingerbread," I told her. "Frankie, Theo, Kim, and me had already worked it out as a potential back up plan. It made more sense for me to attend with Frankie who could do magic, coax out my powers or tell me spells if needed, than with my boyfriend. I'm sorry we couldn't tell you, but you kind of can't be trusted."

"I understand. But I hope now I'm out of Hell and away from Satan's instructions we can try to be civil," Lucy said. "I'm going to go now. Your mother will no doubt appear at any moment and like I said, I'm sick of seeing your father's face." She sliced her arm through the air and then turned to me. "Forgot I can't do that anymore. Looks like I'm walking. Time to find somewhere to stay." With that she walked out of the room.

Theo arrived with Kim shortly afterwards. He looked around his burned-out apartment. "Kim's been checked out at the hospital and she's fine," he said. "Looks like I need to find that sire of mine so I can move into the farm."

"I'm afraid Satan killed your sire years ago, so

you're not going to get that debt settled," I told him. "And don't even think about looking for your sire's, sire's, sire. The farms bought now. End of."

"Ugh. Well at least technically you bought it." He harrumphed, then looked around. "Where's Frankie? I'd like to thank him for protecting my future wife," he said, and I began to sob. "He died." I told him. "Saving my life."

"Died?" he said. "How long since the time of death?"

"About thirty minutes," I said. "What does it matter? I've lost my friend and what am I going to tell Kim?" Kim was currently standing next to Darius. They were doing the weird staring at each other thing again. He was filling her in on things and it was only a matter of time until he got to the part about Frankie.

Theo leapt away from me and into the bedroom. I ran after him. He latched onto Frankie's neck and began to suck.

"You can't do that! That's disgusting. I know he's dead and can't feel it but for fuck's sake, Theo, put him down, you sick bastard."

I dived into my handbag, pulled out a plastic Tupperware box and started throwing pieces of steak at him.

Kim burst through the door. "He's dead. Oh God, he's dead." She took one look at his charred body and ran back out heaving.

Theo glared at me. "Can you stop throwing food at me – again? And we'll be having a conversation about why you're walking around with steak in your bag when we get home. I'm not draining him. We have a one-hour window for me to bring him back. He'll be a vampire, and will have lost his magical powers on death, but he'll be able to guide you. He just won't be able to perform magic himself anymore. Do you think he'd want that? To be undead rather than not be here anymore?"

"Yes," said a female voice. My mother came through the doorway. "He's a very dear friend and between us we'll show him there's a new path for him. Please, turn him." Theo slit his wrist with a small knife he took from his pocket and let his blood fall into Frankie's mouth. After the first few drops, Frankie's body began to heal and his mouth fixed on Theo's wrist, where he sucked like his life depended on it, which it totally did. After a few minutes, Theo pushed him away and licked the puncture marks to close the wound.

"I'll take him," said my mother. "Myself and Dylan will take him to the caves until he has learned to master his new strength." Theo nodded.

"We will speak soon, daughter," my mother said, giving me a kiss on the cheek. "But for now, rest up and take care of your friend. It's been quite an eventful evening."

I nodded, and she left.

Theo and I walked out of the room and back to Kim. Darius was with her in the bathroom. She crouched over the toilet, looking pale and wan.

"I can't believe he died."

"He didn't," I told her.

"You mean that overcooked chip is still alive?" she asked, her eyes wide. "That's even worse. No amount of *Extreme Makeover* can fix that."

"He's back to looking like himself, although much, much paler. Theo turned him and saved his life."

"He's not dead?" she asked.

"Err, yeah, he's pretty dead, well, pretty undead."

"Oh," she said. "Well I don't think I can date him anymore because I'll keep seeing Chargrilled Charlie." She vomited again.

"I'll get you some water and then we need to all go to my house." I looked around the burned-out shell. "I don't know what these devils have against soft furnishings."

Chapter Eighteen

Shelley

It took a few days for us all to come to terms with the effects of Halloween. Kim was being monitored by a doctor at the local hospital who specialised in supernatural cases. I'd met him and he was both human and fantastic looking but Kim had no interest.

"I need time out from dating," she told me as we sat in Jax's waiting for the other businesswomen to join us. "In the last couple of weeks, I've learned Withernsea is full of supernaturals, had a near-death experience, and a boyfriend who went from wizard to fledgling vampire and is currently locked away for his own safe-keeping."

"They have to do that when they're new or they do what Theo did."

She sighed. "I know. He's called me you know. He says it's changed him, and although he remembers who he was, it's not who he is now. But we're going to try to be friends when he eventually comes out."

"It's a shame. I can highly recommend having a vampire boyfriend."

"I've already told you that she's destined for the shifter," Ebony's voice came from behind us. "But not for a while." She stroked Kim's face. "You look pale. You must rest, and in the meantime, my cosmetics are fully stocked up so you can look less wan. I'll put a compact to one side for you."

"Seriously? I'll be okay?" Kim asked.

"Yes. Well, there might be a few little hiccups in your path but it'll work out."

"What hiccups?" yelled Kim. "Like being half drained to death?"

"I'll just get my coffee ordered," Ebony said, walking towards Jax.

"I'm going off her," Kim said.

"Well, I need to talk to you. You know my deal with Satan. I agreed to not run the Supernatural Dating Agency."

"I know. What's going to happen now? I'm no use at anything else. Do you think the new owners will keep me on?"

"You're such a dumb cow sometimes. You're going to run it – if you're willing of course. I'll do the humans and you do the supes. If there's any crossover you'll have to manage it. I'm bound by my pact, I can't match make."

"Does that mean a pay rise?" she asked, smiling and winking.

"Yes, it does, and longer, less flexible hours."

"That's fine. I'm going to be a workaholic instead of a sexaholic."

I rolled my eyes.

Jax and Ebony joined the table, shortly followed by Samara from the groomers and finally Lucy.

"Everyone, this is Lucy," I introduced her.

"Hi again. Cute headband," said Jax.

"I said that too," said Samara.

"It's a great signature look," added Ebony. "They're from my boutique." She winked at Lucy whose floral headband was styled to cover up the two small protrusions that remained on her head.

"So, Lucy was just telling me she opened a steakhouse near the promenade," said Samara.

"Yes." Lucy nodded. "Barbecue is my speciality."

I went into my bag and brought out some cards. "You're all invited," I told them.

Kim shrieked. "You're getting married?! How did he propose? Tell us all."

"Well," I said. "It was Thursday evening and Theo and I were in the bedroom. We'd decided that cuddling each other made us feel much better after recent events and then well, anyway..."

"Is there a point to this or are you showing off that you're having sex?" sniped Lucy.

"Anyway, afterwards we lay in each other's arms and I realised that after everything that had happened, I didn't want to wait. Also, I apologised for jumping to conclusions several times, and well, everything was just, at that moment, perfect." I sighed. "Then we both said it, at the same time. 'Will you marry me', and then we both said 'yes' at exactly the same time." I beamed. "Then we totally had a ton of hot sex again and yes I'm saying that to rub it in your face, biatch," I told Lucy.

"You realise you have to get me a date, don't you?" she said to Kim.

"That'll be a devil of a date," quipped Kim. "On your application we'll have to put something like raging PMT. No, PHT. Post-Hell tension."

Lucy sneered at her. "I throw out chips that resemble your last date," she bitched. "How is Franken-fried, anyway?"

"Still in training." I said, "and anyway, back to me." I pointed to the invites. We're getting married at the farm – on Monday."

"Monday?" Kim said. "That's a bit soon."

"Well, the guy agreed to move out super-fast," I said, failing to mention that it was because he thought Simon Cowell wanted to move in and he got a photo and an autograph for his helpfulness. "Also, we already have the fireworks on Sunday in the park and I don't want to detract from that. So, Monday it is, for an extra firework party."

Then the *Female Entrepreneurs who do it with their Colleagues* talked about plans for the new year.

"I can't wait to become Mrs Landry," I told Theo. "And I can't believe that I actually have a father to give me away." I'd met up with my parents a couple of times. Although we'd clicked, we were taking it slow. Plus, they'd not seen each other for twenty-six years, so I was keeping well away from their house. My mother had promised to keep teaching me magic and my father to tell me more about being a wyvern. He'd told me that I shared responsibility in keeping 'Wyvernsea' a thriving community.

"And after we have our baby and you're ready, I'll turn you into my vampire wife as well as my wedded wife," Theo said. I had to admit I was nervous about the whole undead, live for hundreds of years thing, but there was no immediate rush.

"Well the fireworks have arrived." Theo said. "So, all we need now is for the day to arrive."

"In the meantime, I do believe fireworks have started right here in my panties." I told my fiancé. "Fancy a bang?"

Of course, our wedding took place on an evening. We

stood in the grounds of our farmhouse, surrounded by family and friends. Even my adoptive parents had attended, along with Polly. Theo and I had decided we preferred to get married on our own land than in a church. I was kept warm by patio heaters and the bonfire. It was alright for my husband, being undead, he didn't feel the cold.

My husband. Gosh it seemed strange to say those words.

But now the last of the guests were leaving, mainly because my best friend was telling everyone that they'd stayed long enough and they needed to fuck off. I don't know who had the worst attitude-her or Lucy.

Speaking of Lucy, I stood in the doorway of my home unseen as she wandered down the driveway towards her taxi. I watched as she flicked her thumb and a flame shot out. She could still shoot fire.

But that was something to think about another day. Right now, it was time for my husband-there was that word again-to carry me over the threshold of our new home, and take me to bed.

"Are you ready, Mrs Landry?" he asked me.

"Yes, Mr Landry. Very ready."

He picked me up, white gown and all, without effort and escorted me over the threshold, placing me down in the hallway. I'd been in close proximity to his body while he carried me and I was ready to be a whole lot closer.

"Welcome home," a wavering voice came from our left.

I turned around and my jaw dropped. There in front of me was the hazy outline of a woman.

"Mum?" said Theo. "Is that you?"

THE END

Read more adventures from Withernsea in A Devil of a Date.

A DEVIL OF A DATE

My best friend made a deal with the Devil...

I now run The Supernatural Dating Agency, a discreet section of Withernsea's finest matchmaking service. Yeah, I'll do all the work while Shelley makes babies with her gorgeous vampire husband.

It's not like I've anything better to do anyway. My ex is now a newly-turned vamp struggling to accept he can no longer admire his own reflection, and I don't care what Ebony 'sees', Kim is *not* about to date a wolf; he has better hair than I do.

Then Lucy Fir, fresh from the gates of guarding Hell, decides she wants me to find her a boyfriend. He'll need to be a Knight in shining inflammable armour with her temper. Can I find her a date, or is my new career damned before it's even started?

Welcome to Withernsea and the Supernatural Dating Agency, for readers of Michelle Rowen, Gerry Bartlett and Michele Bardsley who like their humour to have bite.

Buy A Devil of a Date if you like your romance...HOT.

Andie M. Long is author of *Amazon Number One Erotic Thrillers* **Saviour,** and **The Alphabet Game** amongst others.

She lives in Sheffield with her son and long suffering partner.

When not being partner, mother, employee or writer she can usually be found on Facebook or walking her whippet, Bella.

THE ALPHA SERIES

The Alphabet Game

The Alphabet Wedding

The Calendar Game

The Baby Game

THE BALL GAMES SERIES

Balls

Snow Balls

New Balls Please

Balls Fore

Jingle Balls

Curve Balls

Birthing Balls

STANDALONE TITLES

Underneath

Journey to the Centre of Myself

Saviour

MInE

The Bunk-up (with DH Sidebottom)

Made in the USA
Monee, IL
10 March 2021